New Views

Of Old News

New Views

Of Old News

stories by
Jarrod Campbell

These stories are dedicated to a past that is always repeating and a future that is forever just beyond our reach.

Contents:

Ce n'est jamais qu'à cause d'un état d'esprit qui n'est
pas destiné à durer qu'on prend des résolutions
définitives.

-Marcel Proust

The Colluder

As soon as one relationship ended, another was close enough behind so that I wouldn't go homeless. A habitual co-inhabitant? More like a professional. It was a lifestyle choice I made as soon as I moved out of my parents' house at eighteen. Loneliness or even being alone were both never options. I need someone or something around at all times. If whoever is my boyfriend at the time isn't around, then I'm a friend indeed since I need human face time from when I get up until I go to bed. Otherwise it's a pet that has to put up with me being needy. The more I think about it, I guess my dependency issue is a bigger problem after all. I'm surely the reason why I've gotten to this point.

First and foremost, I naturally blame my parents. I was spoiled rotten even though we didn't have much. My parents made sure I had whatever I wanted and I gladly accepted with no questions asked. Accidentally an only child, I had an older sister who died when I was five. I don't remember her all too well but I do remember she had a great sense of humor and always wanted me around her, whether I was awake or not. To her I must've been an interactive toy. I wondered later if she knew she wouldn't get better, would never grow up and have any children of her own, so she substituted me for what she'd never have. The pictures of her that mom kept as a shrine gave a face to those and the few other memories I have of her. But if those frames mom polished daily weren't around I doubt I would've been able to put a face to a name.

Late Spring would usually bring out the worst in my parents. Francis died in May, that I was never allowed to forget. Mom would get madder than ever at the littlest disagreement between her and dad, especially any involving me. It wasn't a secret that she blamed my dad. One year after my sister's passing, my mom was more drunk than normal and told me he could have done more to save her. She stopped when I started crying. By then I was old enough to understand the accusation. That's when she made up her mind to protect me from him. But protect me from what? He never posed a threat, physical or otherwise. In retaliation to my mom's devotion to me he did the same but always went one step above her efforts. These little wars

3

thankfully only lasted a few months out of the year until my mom's birthday in late June.

So, when people are wearing pastels and finally white, celebrating birth, renewal, hope and all that happy crap, I'm probably looking for friendly faces and a place to live. My behavior changes in the spring too; I learned from watching my parents. People I've known a while tell me I get irritating and grouchy. This is when I have a hard time keeping boyfriends and sometimes friends. And if I am in a relationship and living with him then it's almost automatic that I start looking for another place to live.

The relationship I'm in now had an interesting beginning. I went from one guy to another but that wasn't the strange part. I moved immediately from one boyfriend's apartment into another's. And normally I'm the one who's cheated on. They'll say I'm too clingy and jump on the first person who could be just a body and keep the dialogue simple and non-invasive. I've heard that or similar more than once. What hurts the worst about being cheated on is that I never understand since I'm pretty much always ready to have sex. But this time I was the cheater, only because I knew my soon-to-be ex-boyfriend at the time had been cheating since day one of us seeing each other. And he was the one I dated the longest, two whole years.

The time invested made learning about his cheating painful at first. Understandable. He was away on business a lot and found guys on a hook up app to fuck in his fancy all expenses paid company hotel room. So if he could do it and act like he doesn't then so could I. We eventually left each other for guys we liked to fuck and talk to more. I really enjoyed his companionship more than sex anyway and God did he like to talk. This made it easier for me to accept it all in the long run and this is also why we stayed friends.

After him I immediately moved in with S_. I had the advantage of getting to know him during the last year of my previous relationship. He is genuinely kind, caring and completely in love with me. I can do nothing wrong. The first year of us living together was an adjustment. It came from him living alone for a while and also from my being used to a certain standard in a relationship. Probably my biggest complaint is that I had to take on practically all of the cleaning duties, otherwise I'd have to go to bed with a sink full of dishes every night.

Once we came to certain understandings and expectations were discussed then confirmed, things ran much smoother. S_ and I cosigned on the apartment together so I felt I was entitled to an equal say in how things might be and he agreed. Every truce was made without argument or attitude, I would like to add. That's how our relationship continued. I didn't mind doing more housework if it meant I wouldn't have to worry about finding a new place to live when spring rolled around.

Another year together came and went without any real incident. Sure there were usual disagreements about music in the car or what to watch on TV and frequent lectures about why I shouldn't balance ladders on stairs when attempting my constant home improvements but that was it. Nothing of note. This was definitely something I wasn't used to. Even Spring came and went without so much as a resentful glance from either of us. Having no excuses, plans or little white lies to occupy my mind I had more time to think. I even started spending a small amount of each day completely alone and without my cell phone so I could think in peace.

These moments of withdrawal didn't go unnoticed by S_. In a lot of regards he's like me. The major similarity is that he doesn't like to spend time alone. Several of his friends would call and he would go out, or have company over, but nothing regular. Once I happened to be around and watch them all interact. His friends seemed more like a chore for him to get out of the way. I would constantly encourage him to hang out with other people whenever he wanted but he would say no and ask me what I felt like doing that day instead. After a while I gave up.

One day, not that long ago really, everything changed. If my memory is reliable then the time was on a recent day off of work, around six in the evening. Knowing S_ would be coming home around that time, I started making a basic pasta dinner, a staple of my limited abilities in the kitchen. This wasn't uncommon behavior. I often cleaned during my day off if S_ had to work and I tried to make sure he came home to a meal, especially if I had been home all day. It was the least I could do, really. What if, I began to think as I heard the horn announce that S_ had locked his car doors remotely – what if he decided to leave me? No reason in particular made me think that, just suddenly it was there in my head, fully formed.

The standard reaction would be to have a friend lined up with an available room. The friends we did have dropped off since we both worked so much and barely had time for anybody else but ourselves. The rest had quickly disappeared when I managed to piss them off in some way or other. Any friends S_ and I shared were certainly out of the question. Even though they were the most ignored they remained more loyal to him than any of my friends did to me.

"How was your day?" I asked automatically, just as I would've any other Monday through Friday. And, just like any other weekday after work, S_ would recap all the senseless shit he had to deal with over the last eight hours. I was only half-listening while he talked and I finished making dinner. Then, out of nowhere and way out of the ordinary, he walked into the kitchen and kissed me long and passionately. A polite kiss was usually exchanged when one of us greeted the other but that evening it didn't happen. Was this why he felt like he needed to make a big production out of what was normally a passing action?

"No," S_ said, "I just wanted to kiss you like that out of the blue...keeps you on your toes. Besides, it's been a while." What he said was true. What he said also made me suspicious. He was a creature of habit like me and I know I wouldn't do something like that without good reason. His purpose I wasn't buying. And I damn sure wouldn't say anything like that. What the hell do I need to be prepared for? After two years together, our routines were already firmly set and the first kiss of greeting had always been a quick kiss on the lips. I admit that I worry too much and let my mind run wild but the more I thought about it and the longer I watched him for the rest of the evening I could tell his brain was also running a mile a minute.

That night I couldn't sleep. Neither could S_. So we did what two people in bed do when neither could sleep. After a couple years of being together, the intensity of sex could vary but I don't remember that much passion between his legs since the very beginning. As much as I enjoyed it, the only lasting effect was more suspicion. There was no prompt or real reason, as far as I could tell. I even jokingly asked if I had overlooked our anniversary, mostly for my own sake, to make sure I didn't genuinely forget. S_ ended up sleeping very well that night while I, on the other hand, didn't sleep a wink since all I could do was worry. I counted sheep, I counted S_'s snores but when the sun started to rise I just got up as usual and lied when asked how I slept.

Sleeping for shit makes you look like shit and I knew it was written all over my face. S_ humored me and went along with it, always all smiles. Given my way of thinking, I felt his response to my fibbing only added to my belief that he was cheating on me. Having been cheated on before I didn't really care about that part. I was more afraid that I was going to be evicted. There was nobody else to move in with and I came to realize that more importantly I didn't want to live with anybody else.

From then on, he was even more clingy than usual. If we went to a bookstore, he would follow me. When I was tired and felt like I needed to go to bed early, then he would say he was also tired and follow me upstairs. I became aware that he was always attached to my hip so I would test him: walking fast in stores deliberately trying to lose him or insisting he stay downstairs and watch something on TV, nothing would ever shake him. Out of frustration I deliberately followed him around in stores, never separating from him unless he had to use the bathroom or try something on. I'm not sure if he got the point or not but one thing came of it.

Guessing whether or not he was cheating on me or going to leave me became easier thanks to what I gathered by staying in such close proximity all the time. Eventually he flat out asked me why I would follow him and never go off by myself when we went to stores. My answer was plain and honest, even if only half-true. I said it's what I thought he wanted, since he was figuratively up my ass all the time.

My response confused him, probably because he could always tell when I was being a jerk and trying to pass my reaction off as rational. S_ never cared for conflict, neither did I. This was something else we had in common. And how he came at me and addressed my behavior was certainly confrontational, but not aggressive. He didn't care about holding anything in; for him to blurt out like he did was out of character. Thankfully he kept his composure and didn't yell since I'm not sure how well I would have been able to take being yelled at by him.

I knew that my hunch was right. S_ explained how he thought that I was getting sick of him which is why I had been wanting more time alone. He confessed that he thought it would be a good idea to turn up the charm, to use his words. Insisting that was the only reason, I believed him and proved it with a genuinely sincere hug and kiss. I felt this was necessary for both our sakes: for S_ it excused my past behavior and served as a better version of a handshake over an agreement to never do anything stupid again. For me it was necessary to help hide what I was afraid my face was sure to give away.

S_ and I share similarities, as I've already mentioned. We were born exactly one month apart. There was something growing in S_ that I recognized as a part of myself. This exasperation was something I could only see when looking inward. Perspective made me understand how I must have come across to so many people. Co-dependency was somewhat understandable and often the norm considering where we live but maybe we were taking it too far.

Having no friends was also telling of how horribly I'm seen by other people. I thought for sure that my neediness would be a problem but it seemed to only endear me to S_ even more as a perfect compliment for his need to have and to hold. This worked well for him which is why I guessed he embraced my parasitic nature and overreacted when I started spending more and more time alone. I promised him it was only to think and I'm sure he understands that to be the truth. But my thoughts turned more personal and rarely ever addressed anybody else's needs or feelings. And since I'd been abandoned by everybody I know except the person I was living with, this made it easy to put all the focus inward.

What on earth could he possibly see in me? I've asked this question so much that it took over my ability to think about much else. I am mediocre. I never excelled in school and clearly wasn't planning on being anything above average in life. In my opinion there was no reason to be madly in love with me at all, let alone stick with me for so long. I could understand the convenience of my previous ex keeping me around, it was for the sake of appearances and his parents, bless their hearts. But for S_ to want me still was baffling. What could I possibly offer an overachiever like him?

Nothing, I concluded. Fortunately, he was out running errands when I had the "come to Jesus" moment because I became hysterical and cried when it hit me. With so much to give, I feel it is being wasted on me and originally intended to tell him so. But the more I think about it, the more I know he'll try and probably succeed in talking me out of it. Even if I promise a clean break up, he'll try to stop me from leaving. S_ doesn't like confrontation or change and since I don't either he'd probably also use that to his advantage. He would win his case by reminding me I had no other place to go and nobody else to stay with. And I would lose my nerve only to stay and go on like before, always just floating. But I couldn't stand that I was making him as awful as I must have always been to everybody I've ever known. One was enough. Two will be insufferable.

So, this drastic conclusion was reached. Here I sit, patiently waiting on a ladder behind the basement door. There's a vague timeframe when S_ will be home with the gallons of purified water we store at the foot of the stairs. I set up the ladder over an hour ago and have been sitting here thinking what I hope will happen. I'm impressed that my mind isn't racing or I don't have a headache, at least. All I can think about is how happy he will be when I'm gone. The shock of accidentally killing me would wear off; he could convince himself it was my own fault, especially considering how often he told me to not be on a ladder, on the stairs and by a door. When it no longer keeps him up at night, he'll be much better off, I know it. No more worrying if I loved him or not or if I was going to leave him. And for me, no more agonizing

15

over if he would ever leave me. In a way, we're kind of doing each other a favor, more or less.

New Vistas, Inside and Outside

It was not the idea of change that scared him.

His whole life, Eddie found himself uprooted then

shuffled off to another relative who would eventually

decide an extra mouth to feed was more than they

originally bargained for. It certainly was not the idea of

settling down that scared him, either. A routine and

stable life was all he ever wanted as far back as he could

remember. What scared Eddie was the city. He saw it as

constantly bustling and always intoxicated by its own

energy and excess. The noise, above all, was the worst.

He appreciated a certain serenity that a bucolic

upbringing and existence could provide. Eddie preferred

simplicity, silence and stability. The city offered none of

this but so much more. A better job. Higher salaries.

An encouraging future. Should clarity of mind, body and

soul be comfortably traded for convenience? Could these

and other apprehensions be calmed by love?

When he and his wife moved to the city, Eddie

had just come back from the war. There, the sameness

and uniformity were dreadful; sandy dunes and endless

desert as far as all eyes could see. An empty terrain

spotted with armored metal machines was more

disconcerting without the presence of any trees. It was the only time an absence of noise upset him. Loud noises in that world were the sound of the actual tearing of that flimsy curtain between life and death. Some changes were easily dealt with, others were far more challenging. Still, he found the city to be more overwhelming.

Pulling back one of the drapes, he looked outside at his new world through the high-rise window. His reflection could be clearly seen in the glass, creating the illusion that he was floating above the cars and people. An anxious fear moved him back a few feet from the window. Now he appeared to be standing on the top of a neighboring building. Eddie had once opened that other thin curtain and seen what light and wonder waited on the other side. A miracle made him the only one from a group of twenty that came back from behind the curtain. He returned with a titanium souvenir from the right knee down and a blue hue added to the red of his heart.

He had considered this a small change compared to the more recent uprooting and replanting in concrete. "How can you hate some place you've never been?" his wife would ask any time he would so much as grumble. There was no abundance of trees near where they lived, only the occasional sapling perfectly imprisoned in its individual cement plot. These cheerless excuses for nature were never satisfactory even when clustered closer together. And always, non-stop, was the noise. People were forever laughing, shouting, crying or cursing. He believed the constant sirens were a warning that the city was perpetually in danger of killing itself. With all of the fires reported endlessly on the news it was further proof for him that the candle was being burned not just at two ends but several, and quickly.

Yet each morning the sun would rise again upon the city to share its glory or the rain would be merciful and come rinse away its dirt and sin. And with the dawn, the noise – rising and falling with the rhythm of the day – would resume. Severe headaches would come on and he could think of nothing clearly for very long. Poor decisions were made during these times and Eddie was afraid that he might be choosing the worst verdict of his life. He had to be able to think clearly but he could never filter out the cacophony that rose up from the streets.

Samantha came home most days a half hour or so after Eddie. This gave him enough time to change out of his work clothes and shower. He came to see this half hour as a personal refuge from the outside world at large. The dimensions of the bathroom were not small but cozy enough. It was his sanctuary tucked away in the middle of the apartment. The hot shower and the resulting steam fogging the mirrors thawed his bones. And from this cocoon he would emerge every evening wiped of the city's grimy fingerprints once again.

Daily interaction with people was deliberately kept to a minimum: a few coworkers, a few folks at the coffee shop and Samantha. Managing a team of nearly two hundred people, she came home each day with unbelievable stories of human hubris and ignorance. These did more harm by reassuring Eddie that the creation of noise would be constant. The people responsible for his wife's own hurdles were out there and undoubtedly also responsible for his own. Every day these stories compounded evidence to convince the one-man jury that he did not belong in the hive of a metropolis. A voice began buzzing more prominently, rising above the others with a faint but singular message serving as a reminder of how Eddie was different and how he should not become indifferent only to eventually give in and stay. A month saw this voice roaring to the point he wondered if his love for Samantha would be enough to make him accept a jail of concrete, glass and booming sound.

One sweltering day in July, high temperatures intensified the sedative results of the accompanying humidity. Eddie commonly felt the relieving heat as another buffer against the commotion outside that he knew was slowly scaling the walls of the high-rise to steal inside the locked glass balcony door. In spite of the daily shower he could not seem to get rid of the grime from the city's grubby hands. Frustration and irritation could linger and stain but only if this residue remained.

Just out of the shower, the door halfway opened, Eddie saw Samantha dressing down after what was assuredly a ridiculous day. Exasperation was evident in her breathing and also in the fidgety way she undressed. She barely noticed the door open or Eddie's exit and only finally acknowledged him a mere foot or so from her performance. They both forced a smile and their kiss was unusually light and slightly off center. Immediately after their clumsy and careless lips separated, Samantha launched into telling him how he would not believe the day she had. Eddie did not even have to ask, he never had to ask. He stopped listening before the beginning of her second sentence. Looking his wife up and down his mind drifted to why he had initially been attracted to her and fell in love since very little had physically or emotionally changed since they first met. But the tone of her voice always transformed as she ranted through the happenings of her day. "Are you listening to me?" Samantha must have repeated several times judging from the look of impatience that wrinkled her forehead. Eddie's response was to turn around and walk out of the bedroom.

23

Samantha knew by that point in their relationship to not take this behavior personally and to give him space; he would come to her when he was more prepared and capable to converse and interact. Absentmindedly following him out after a pause she found him sitting on the couch in the living room. This intrusion was not met with enthusiasm, but Samantha persisted. Opening her mouth to speak, the attempt was stifled by a scream from an over-stimulated Eddie. It was an expression of rage, of weariness from a panic of never truly being heard and of the dread of being swallowed then forgotten under an encroaching and devastating wave of noise. Two more followed after a recovery breath from the one before and their intensity, ebbed with each issue yet retained a heightened level of defeat.

Embarrassed when he realized his actions visibly frightened his wife, he quickly got to his feet then walked to the window. There was hesitation for a moment before Eddie pulled back the curtains. The city's racket scratched and banged on the glass window; these laughs, cries, shouts and curses. He was anxious and terrified of being broken from the warring sounds outside and the aggressive atmosphere. Without turning to look at Samantha to show worry on his face, he called her name. In an instant, Samantha went to Eddie and met him with an embrace from behind, her arms around his torso and her right cheek nestled in his back. His breathing was quick and nervous, unsure. Every inhalation made his wife's grip lightly tighten which imbued his exhalations with the soothing influence of her body.

When his breathing became steadier and relaxed Eddie noticed how he had become very aware of Samantha's heartbeat as well as his own. More startling was the realization that for every two times her heart beat he would either make one full inhalation or exhalation. Feeling and understanding this connection to the woman he loved had the most encouraging effect of all. And with this new calm came further awareness, additional initiations. For a certain number of breaths, a traffic light below the window would stay red. Wanting to see exactly just how deep this linking went his attention turned to his wife's breathing. For every set number of full breaths, a specific number of people walked through a crosswalk. Staring down at the stop light for a moment he saw a red light turn green. The traffic and physical movement began again in one direction and stopped the intersecting direction, facilitating the city's circulation of vehicles and pedestrians. This ebb and flow of activity was vital to keeping everything operational and alive, nourished and wounding without partiality. An abstract smile slowly turned up the corners of his mouth. Easier now to believe in the interrelation of everything, Eddie knew he had observed further evidence of a deeper and more reciprocal relationship to his new home and city.

With the last of the sunlight hastily leaving the sky, Samantha and Eddie kept their hold unbroken until the final rays disappeared. The living room was dark, and this blackness brought a stillness to them both. "I should probably turn on a light," Samantha whispered before squeezing Eddie once more and let him go to follow through with her suggestion. With the light turned on, Eddie's reflection again appeared in the glass as though he were floating above the city in the night sky. The lights from the streets and the cars reflected back as stars. And when his wife rejoined him, they became a part of this illusory universe together. The darkly colored parts of their clothing blended into the black of the streets and night, making parts of their disjointed anatomy enhance or embrace other pieces of architecture.

Eddie turned and looked at Samantha in the reality of the dimly lit living room. He was glad that her face no longer appeared troubled and her near serene expression suggested that he too must at last seem composed. As much as his mouth wanted to smile, the urge to kiss Samantha was stronger and won. The connection was felt again. Ultimately their heartbeats, though differing in tempo, echoed and further drove the pulse of a city that no longer upset Eddie. The noise – the ever-present laughing, crying, shouting, cursing – they were his and they were hers. The upturned sides of his mouth were an approval and acceptance that they belonged to everybody else as well.

Sheila, I'm Coming Over

Sheila I'm coming over

It was a simple enough text to convey his intention. There would be nothing simple about the conversation; the reason he needed to come to her place. The outcome would be easy to deal with but the unavoidable road there might be rough. To prepare, she thought of replies for questions that were sure to be asked. Sheila wanted to be well-rehearsed so that her nimble responses would give further credibility to her act. If love was to be played as a game then she preferred to have the odds in her favor.

Hopefully, Sheila thought as she surveyed her small apartment, *he takes it well and doesn't throw anything*. The contemplation was valid and finished right as her stare fell on a spot near a closet. Newer white paint covered an accident and was still slightly brighter than the rest of the wall. Nothing was thrown but the wall was kicked hard when one guy did not appreciate the flippancy with how their relationship ended. That guy had a bad temper whereas the man on his way over was much more subdued. Reflex still moved her sights to the corner of the room by the couch where she kept a wooden bat. Another box ticked from her mental checklist.

Jeremy was a good guy, she surmised. There were no noticeable unappealing physical qualities, in fact he was well put together. Sheila had yet to see him naked after two weeks of dating and this was a decision he sincerely honored. Jeremy was genuinely nice. He never let her pay for a meal, always listened intently when she spoke and even opened doors for her. The final reason for ending their relationship was embarrassingly silly since so many good things were in place. In light of such chivalry Sheila knew she would be ridiculed by her friends, probably even by Jeremy. Holding fast to her decision was easy once she believed her reasons were justified.

While checking the time, the text appeared again on the screen. *Sheila I'm coming over.* Only six minutes had passed since the initial reception of the message. Twenty minutes until the end of her current relationship she attempted to use her nervous energy to productive ends. The problem was that Sheila did not believe in loose ends; there were no dishes to be done, no laundry that needed folding or even emails that needed checked.

She could go stir crazy if her only option was to sit and wait while her brain searched for preoccupation. Television could be senseless and mind numbing so she turned on the set. The first thing that appeared was a man and woman kissing passionately before they took each other's clothes off to make love. Changing the channel she found no reprieve: a gum commercial where a woman proved the freshness of her breath by kissing her husband. That was enough. Sheila knew that her books could offer no sanctuary. Those tastes tended towards the improbably romantic and any movie she would want to watch always ended happily ever after with a kiss.

A kiss. It was inescapable, thinking of her first kiss with Jeremy. What started with an amazing sensation was about to end with an exchange of words and an absolute severing of emotions. Easy as that, she anticipated. Feelings were stirred as she allowed herself to remember one last time. Knowledge of how that story was going to end made for a more facile completion, Sheila sighed. Every kiss that followed steadily lost bits of a magic that was present and fully formed within the first, only to be fragmented and shattered completely the night before by a conclusive, mediocre kiss.

There were many things Sheila wanted and would like to be. Dreams were still clear and believable at her age and not once during their couple week courtship did Jeremy ever visit her sleep. While awake she could not afford to be showy or care about what people might think about her nice clothes bought cheap from a sales rack. But in her inner world at night her reveries had more than once been populated with fancy soirees and glass slippers. Jeremy never appeared at any party in any role, major or minor. Sheila was brought up to believe in fairy tale endings fit for upper middle-class princesses. Dad said it would be so his whole life. That is what he gave his wife, her mother, and that is what most certainly was in the cards for her.

Her dad, who worked hard for everything they ever had, knew how to treat his wife. Their parts seemed instinctual. A veritable queen in a king's castle, her every whim and fancy was catered to and in return she offered her devotion. Mom managed the house dad paid for and she matched domestically his fervor for providing. Fairytale princesses in pale blue gowns longed for and found the exact kind of love she knew her parents shared. Very early on in her life, the movies she grew up watching validated her beliefs. There was always a magical kiss and Sheila grew up believing that this magic never died. Proof again came from her mother's elation anytime her husband so much as kissed her cheek. In turn, Sheila envied her mother for having in real life what belonged to her princess heroines. Behind the scenes were never shown or made known to Sheila; the missing pieces of the puzzle kept the bigger picture incomplete. The illusion was a result, the sum of many days full of contrasting miracles and fluctuating kilowatts of electricity. Each day became a small part of an enchanting whole.

Jeremy and his handsome princely features lacked the magic to miraculously whisk her from the drudgery of reality. The trappings of royalty accompanied him and his inheritance could create and sustain new, more impressive fantasies. Without the charm from a kiss however, he could never fully claim and fill her empty heart. After every kiss goodnight Sheila would rush upstairs to her apartment and noticeably shrink with dismay when her reflection lacked the glow her mother radiated every time her lips touched those of her true love. Sheila swore she understood by feeling something enigmatic whenever her father kissed her goodnight.

A quick glance at her phone alerted her that soon the blighted relationship would all be over. It startled her that more time had passed than she thought. Anxiety was scarce. Concentration on life after their break up made any straggling remnants of remorse float away on the backs of the effusive notes from a Chopin etude drifting from well hidden speakers. A smile began to alter the serenity of her face and Sheila promptly remembered how non-chalance during the last break up altered one of the apartment walls. By the time Jeremy texted his arrival and parked his car, she was prepared; stone faced and stone hearted, ready to do what she knew was the right thing to do.

"Why stay on a sinking ship?" Sheila tried to reason, but Jeremy was relentless. "But you haven't told me why you think the ship is sinking," he replied. Immediately when she looked at his face Sheila began to doubt whether or not to be truthful and say why. Not from a change of heart; she still felt strongly about her reasoning. The hesitation was from the threat of being misunderstood. There was no fear of violence but she did fear his laughter. Would it sound ridiculous to everybody else but her? More than likely, Sheila assumed. A man, in particular, could never understand.

"There hasn't been any magic in any of our kisses since the very first one," Sheila practiced saying a couple of times in her head. Concluding that there was no clearer way to say it, she spoke the sentiment out loud. Jeremy paused before responding. "What do you mean?" he asked. Evidently a man could not understand

36

a basic concept of romance. It was all the proof she needed to successfully write him off. "Are you going to explain?" Jeremy demanded to know, tearing Sheila from her internalizing. "No" was her plain reply, "I don't think I should have to." Jeremy's irritation was written on his face and affected his posture as well. Was what she said real? Was this what he could come to expect from most women his age, right out of college, brimming with implausible ideals? He narrowed his eyes while mulling over Sheila's response.

Standing awkwardly still while waiting for Jeremy to either speak or leave, Sheila studied his expressions and it became clear that he was preoccupied with processing what she had just told him. This granted her a few extra moments to stare at him wholly one last time. Surely he was the most handsome young man she had dated. Certainly he was the wealthiest. And the more she thought about it, Jeremy was also the nicest and most considerate guy she had the pleasure of dating. With those attributes aligned in one person she hoped he could be the perfect man for her, but with no enchantment he would never be able to guarantee the impractical forever she was promised.

Blinking rapidly, Jeremy forced a smile and stared silently towards the door. Relieved by the lack of a scene Sheila made no move to stop him. But something began to bug her and quickly it nagged her to action. *That's it?* she thought. *He can walk away and not even bother to turn around one final time, or at least say goodbye or anything?* "Jeremy wait" Sheila said and walked towards him.

His sudden stopping and spinning around startled her, halting and disrupting her momentum. But nothing worried her more than the look on his face. There was a sign of intention showing in his eyes and also a shift in his stance. From his new position it was easy for him to rush upon her and firmly grab her by the shoulders. Sheila's eyes grew wide with fear at the strength of his grip and also at how completely helpless she felt. Squeezing tighter and pulling her towards him, Jeremy pressed his lips firmly to hers, effectively stifling an arising scream.

The tenderness of his lips softened her firmly clenched mouth before being completely coaxed open by a prying tongue. Within moments her own tongue loosened and mirrored the enthusiasm of the intruder. Sheila felt a warmth wash over her entire body all at once. The heat was most intense in her mouth where the co-mingling of life and breath was strongest. Unquestionably this is how her mother must have felt. Light-headed, her knees buckled and gave out from underneath her. Jeremy expertly caught then cradled her without a break in their embrace.

Wanting to envelope herself in the commotion of Jeremy's kiss, Sheila was expected to suddenly support her own weight. Her lips and shoulders were released from any contact with his mouth and hands. Uncontrollably she felt an urge to be in Jeremy's arms again. Only regret came to prevail along with her balance. Guilt and a need for penitence arose when she watched as he turned around a second time to walk away, not once turning around to take a last look or plead for another chance. In fact his glance never wavered from directly in front of him as he opened the door, walked out and pulled it closed behind his back.

Reversed Racism

The highway was always a nightmare during evening rush hour. Connecting two other major east and west arteries made it integral to thousands of commuters and easier to congest. A simple one-mile stretch could take upwards of thirty minutes or more to drive. With time like that and nowhere to go, radio had a wider audience, particularly with owners of older cars.

In a large white pickup truck every morning and evening, Monday through Friday, Joshua was a commuter at the mercy of talk radio. Popular music was garbage to him, even more so than people talking about how the world is destroying itself. Always on the news were all the horrible things people were doing, either domestically or abroad. America was again threatening to be racially divided. Bigoted white policemen were rampantly shooting unarmed black men and children. Riots were erupting across the country. The government could not be bothered to even address the festering wound that has not been healed for over two hundred years and probably never would.

This quandary worried Joshua for a variety of reasons. Minorities were under the threat of backlash solely for the color of their skin, their religion or gender. The menace was real and always looming. For white people, the looming fear of reverse racism was ever present and to them it was just as real and imposing. Understanding now what minorities must have endured woke some enlightened whites up and made them even more aware and guilty of their privilege.

Politics should be kept private and yes, of course he knew the world was becoming a more appalling place every day, still every show tested Joshua's patience and loathing of top forty radio. The police were getting off without reprimand and washing from their hands the blood spilled in American streets, running off onto everything and becoming a poison whose effect was making up minds so that they could more easily take sides.

The radio shows' topics all week were about all the police shootings and racism. In light of another not guilty verdict, everybody on both sides of the argument

43

had a lot to say. And Joshua could see the rationality
with both views, which left him even more confused and
indecisive about the verdicts. The constant back and
forth about who to blame was becoming as endless as
the last of his time on the highway before his exit. He
believed it added at least ten more minutes to the
commute, regardless of the clock's denial.

Thinking turned to how he would react in
situations involving the unfair treatment of a minority
should he ever be witness to such a thing. If there were
only words being said by one party against another, it
would be fairly easy for him to politely ask the person to
stop. His imposing size and booming voice would be his
reinforcement, so long as the aggressor was not bigger. If
both parties were yelling at each other, Joshua would
more than likely still interject verbally and hope his size
would lend some weight to his request that they stop.

What would he do if the assault switched from
verbal to physical? Would his stature be enough to
impose any real threat? Would he even stick around long
enough to find out? A lifetime of having no aggressive

nature, not even a desire to excel or compete, made Joshua a passive participant in life, a veritable gentle giant. His great height and accompanying weight made most think twice about angering him but would it be a benefit to him if he attempted to use it against somebody who is already angry? He could not effectively fight anybody, so he never did and also never tried.

A commercial was playing when Joshua's focus went back to the radio and the jingle for a fast food restaurant made him return to his previous thoughts. An advertisement for a new church followed. Music and messages of goodwill towards men informed his thinking. Violence was all around, even in his city. How much longer until it affected his neighborhood? Could he use his body as more than a threat, more like a weapon? Taking a punch, shielding somebody innocent from any manner of attack – these were not things he was able to definitively confirm the fortitude to perform.

The possibility of any of these things became unsettling to Joshua. Laughter from the radio alerted him that the commercial break had ended and the debate had resumed. So much time had passed since the debate began at the top of the hour and yet nobody was any closer to agreeing, understanding or forgiving. There would be no salve for this wound, as usual. An impasse was reached on the radio right when Joshua turned off the highway and onto his exit. The silence from switching off the radio and driving away from the endless string of traffic was welcomed and appreciated.

The day was affected by typical hot summer weather but the evening offered a break from the sweltering sun as it began to set. More people began walking when the temperature dropped. Young and old, it delighted Joshua to see people being active. Families of three or more were the usual unit but it was also not uncommon to see a solitary pedestrian. As the T at the end of the road came into view a quarter of a mile away, he did see something unusual. Between Joshua and the end of the road were two men beating up a third while a fourth was lying still on the sidewalk. The third and still somewhat upright man on the ground was being kicked more effectively than he was punched but was still bested by the aggressors.

Chills ran up Joshua's spine as he decelerated his truck by about ten miles per hour. The scuffle involved two brown men, possibly middle-eastern, assaulting a white man. Instinct told him to just drive by, to mind his own business; a flashback to his previous assessments. Human nature told him to help someone in need. Rationality reminded him of the violence already present. But it was an obligation he felt for the victim that won out and compelled him into action.

Not sure of what weapons the attackers may have, Joshua thought it best to not get out of his truck. It was hastily decided that he would drive at them with the truck to scare them away, even running them over if that's what he had to do. The truck swerved towards the melee at the last moment before it would have been impossible to effectively careen the vehicle in their direction. Only the attacker who was not actively hitting the victim at the time of the action ran and jumped from the path of the truck as it drove off the road and onto the double-wide walkway. The other attacker was bunted by the truck several feet into a patch of tall, un-mowed grass.

Stepping out of the vehicle, Joshua immediately ran and assessed the victim. He was conscious and responsive but visibly injured and in considerable pain. Refusing help, the man slowly picked himself up, only to stand stationary and stare at the motionless heap of a person nearby. A grimace crumpled his face, interrupting his daze as he summoned up whatever strength was left in his battered body to kick the immobile form. The blow appeared to hurt the recipient less than its sender. The body only moved under the force of the assault, neither before or after. Nodding an affirmation at a stunned Joshua, the man slowly turned and limped away in the direction of the apartments.

...

"What are you doing walking in the street?" Ishaan was asked three times before his startled brain could think about anything other than nearly being run over by a car. Slowly he walked along the sidewalk without answering the question. The call he was making was dropped immediately after the horn honked and the tires screeched. His passive indifference made the housemates swarm angrily around and glare.

All customarily asked if he was okay and once he offered confirmation, their tones changed and their questioning went from concerned to irritated, warning about how he could have been killed. "You know how Americans drive, especially around here," one of his friends said. "The worst drivers are in America," another offered. With his wits fully about him at last, Ishaan shrugged them off and again began dialing his phone. Attention was paid to the streets and when it was discerned to be clear, he continued walking and talking.

The apartment was buzzing with talk about Ishaan nearly being run over when he returned from his walk. What made it obvious was the abrupt hush his presence caused when he stepped into the kitchen for a glass of water. "I wasn't paying attention, I admit it!" Ishaan snapped. "There are so many more important things to talk about, don't you think?" he demanded to know. The answer was continued silence. "So, nobody can think?" Ishaan mumbled under his breath.

School was going well but he did not have much socialization beyond the confines of the university. The phone call that nearly got him killed was to an academic advisor. A crippling shyness kept him from meeting anybody new, at least in person. Fortunately an app existed so he could meet like-minded people through an electronic filter he felt made him more appealing. A little mystery and a well-angled picture granted him an allure he doubted could be pulled off in person.

Without anything to offer a woman, he understood his situation lended nothing promising to any courtship. Once, an admittedly drunk woman invited him over to her apartment for sex but his lack of mobility prevented that from happening. When she agreed to drive to his place, he had to decline again on account of the people residing at his apartment and the resulting lack of privacy. This missed opportunity was the only prospect during the two months of using the dating app. Fulfilling the utmost priority of female companionship was not coming along as easily for Ishaan as it seemed to be for most everybody else he saw.

A message from a young woman was discovered one morning during breakfast. Ishaan was not sure whether to be excited or suspicious. He had been pranked before and never could understand some people's need to be purposefully cruel. The search for happiness was hard enough without having to also deal with unnecessary malice. But promise always intrigued him so curiosity won out as it always did.

What greeted him seemed genuine. Her name was Heather. Much was discovered shortly after his primary response. An instant attraction was evident and thankfully maintained after their back stories were traded. When it was learned that they lived within close proximity to one another, Ishaan felt more hope than ever about possibly having a girlfriend. A lot was divulged, planned and promised in the five days of their communication.

It was a Tuesday and Ishaan had no classes and the whole day free. The morning was uneventful and so far the afternoon was not the best. The near accident was mentioned to Heather in a text shortly after the call with his school. It was this action that added urgency in Heather's request to finally talk on the phone. Reluctance was always an obstacle but given the recent events and a beautiful woman's insistence, Ishaan relented. Her shift was not over until later in the evening but plans were made to have their inaugural phone call after she was home.

His day was spent trying to have as much time alone as he could. The people and conversation were constant. Even when he had a moment of silence, the clutter of activity never ended and always distracted. Talking to Heather changed all of that. She became a point of intense focus and anything else was easily ignored. When a text conversation ended, the calm in his thoughts and motions lingered enough to become a noticeable change. The narcotic effect was addictive and Ishaan began to need them to maintain what he guessed was normalcy when dealing with stressful situations or other people. One fix could make the lack of privacy and silence a little more bearable.

Anticipating time all day made it take forever to pass just to spite whoever attempted to hurry it along. Ishaan's wait was no different. But finally the hour and phone call came. The call was nearly missed out of a sudden paralyzing panic. Involuntarily, his thumb swiped the bar and the call began. Silence prefaced the conversation once the call was answered. "H-hello..?" Ishaan stuttered. "Hello," came the more assured response from the other line, "nice to finally talk to you." A quick response sputtered out of Ishaan's mouth, followed by more silence. Heather awkwardly continued the conversation and proved with a vocal tic a hardly detectable weak spot in her self-esteem. But Ishaan kept up, even if his first several responses came out as affirmative grunts. Heightened results from Heather were soon pleasantly lowering his level of anxiety. She was just as easy to talk to over the phone as she was in text.

Around the time of Heather's call, the remainder of his roommates began trickling in from their various day jobs. The omnipresent talking and bustle increased and it became more difficult for Ishaan to hear. Walking outside and away from the apartment complex entirely was the only real escape from the commotion. The further away Ishaan walked down the length of the access road that led to the highway, the more the conversation's clarity improved. Strong doses of adrenaline coursed through his veins to promote precision, confidence and better answers.

After carrying the conversation for the first five minutes, Heather asked an open-ended question in order to force Ishaan into speaking. He was ready and able and handled himself very well, much to his own bewilderment. Thankful nevertheless, Ishaan was talking about school and the gratitude he felt about only having less than half a year left. Heather listened intently, seduced by the foreign quality of his accent. While in the middle of sharing his post-graduate plans, the companies he planned on applying to were never said, only interrupted by an audible and agonizing blow to the base of Ishaan's skull.

...

Ordinarily, areas with larger populations were ideal. If a statement needed to be made, why not make it in front of as many people as possible. And should the people witnessing come from a variety of countries, or follow other faiths and politics, the added bonus of international attention was appreciated. Northern Virginia was selected because it had that and more: large, multi-cultural, the close proximity to other major cities...the list was lengthy. Important was the ease one could blend in and be invisible. And given the diversity of the area, nobody ever seemed truly out of place or foreign.

Nationalism seemed inevitable with the rise in vulgar and outspoken hatred parading around as the next wave of progress. It was becoming rampant around the world, especially in the Northern Virginia suburbs of Washington, D.C., which was a microcosm of the world at large. Hiding in plain sight was beneficial when it came to being close to so many enemies, but only if suppressing repulsion and hatred was possible. Groups, gangs, cells: they all existed and flourished in the densely populated suburb of the nation's capital.

Young men like Thomas found the Fighters' Front through other former military sources. In his case it was his bunk-mate from basic training. While deployed in Afghanistan, he had to face fear and death separately in order to shoot the enemy soldier, whose rifle was steadily aimed at Thomas. Every morning and night afterwards, Thomas thanked God that he was able to process fear more effectively than his enemy. Thomas came home with a Purple Heart and blood on his hands. Not knowing what to do after his service, any job became sufficient if the bills were getting paid. A string of temporary girlfriends and empty jobs was his proud legacy and thanks for protecting his country.

Inclusion into a group with a shared disillusionment, similar sense of self-loathing and a communal, eventual hope was a prayer answered. These men experienced nearly everything from similar situations during combat to their subsequent treatment

56

at home by the hands of the unpatriotic. Camaraderie was always instantaneous and after months or years of always feeling misunderstood, loyalties only increased with the greater fear of being unsupported or unwanted. These bonds were fiercely protected at all costs and most would kill to keep them intact, if necessary.

Thomas appreciated his new friends, enough to express interest early on in becoming more involved. Nobody in the group was particularly impressed with him, but no one doubted his enthusiasm and commitment. Persistence assured probable success and after a month of pestering the right people, he was asked to prove his loyalty with a random act of violence. The time, place and target was to be planned by Thomas and presented to a council for approval. If allowed, he would be given the necessary materials and funds before being instructed to proceed.

No time was wasted with Thomas instantly proposing his plan. Wanting to appear more robust and independent in order to surpass the low expectations of him, he proposed simply physically attacking "some

Arabs." When one of his superiors insisted he carry a gun, Thomas felt the requirement was an affront to his diminutive height. This further fueled a desire to succeed and prove his worth. He would take the gun but swore to himself that he would not use it. He did not propose killing anybody and he was not pressed to use a weapon, either. What he offered would be more violent and therefore more newsworthy than just another random shooting.

A compulsion to show the Front what he was made of insisted that he act soon. Executing his attack would be the first moment for him to shine and it would be followed by more shows of devotion. Working his way up through the Fronts' ranks would be truly merit based, unlike another army he once served. Action was the only way to become noticed so Thomas decided the time to act was sooner not later. He felt ready. With no material preparations to be made, Thomas set about readying his mind. Sleep would not be an option that night; accepting that fact was the foremost mental preparation to undertake.

As the sun rose and started filling his room with light, Thomas became aware of his appetite. To keep the body ready it had to have fuel and considering what was being planned, he had the right to treat himself for a change with breakfast from the Tin Diner. Opening the blinds after he got up from the floor where he lay in meditation all night, the fullness of the growing sun heated his skin. It would be warm that day which meant that evening he would have his pick of any one of "them" out walking after dinner. And with the sun setting later it would also ensure walks would last well after he got home from work around six-thirty in the evening.

Wrong in thinking the streets of his apartment complex would be empty at six-thirty in the morning, Thomas noticed a group of young men loitering around a nearby townhouse with the front door wide open. There were too many for the patio to contain so they spilled out into the street. Perpetually on their phones and wandering the neighborhood was common behavior not just for this lot, it was a growing trend. To the old Thomas this just meant more stupid brown people to contend with and tolerate.

Slamming on his breaks startled Thomas as he narrowly avoided hitting a young man on his phone, visibly not paying attention. Fault was shared, a fact the guy realized after flinching at the sound of the screeching car. Misread entirely, Thomas took the apology only as an admission of guilt. Laying on the horn and screaming only furthered the pedestrian's anxious confusion as he hurried out of the street and onto a patch of grass. Slowly the car passed by the pedestrian and four of his friends who by then had gathered to witness the commotion. From inside, the driver pressed his hand, a closed fist with the middle finger extended, against the vehicle's window as it crept past the gawkers.

Diner food could not abate the rage from nearly running over an idiot, Thomas repeatedly thought. And the drive to work was often just as stressful as coming home. Boxes, invoices and boorish salesmen cluttered his day. Deep lines creased his forehead and heavy, dark circles were the effects of his daily grind.

Manual labor was all he was ever hired to do since leaving the service. Employers assumed that he was a grunt in the service so why not let him continue life as a trooper on a sales floor or in a stockroom. His friends would laugh when Thomas said the little bit of his soul that came back with him from Afghanistan was too weak to stand the daily crushing done by working long weeks with barely enough time to breathe. A vacation was a luxury he knew would never be afforded him, regardless of how much he worked.

Thankless jobs paid his bills but offered little else. No satisfaction was ever granted as Thomas simply existed one day in order to live and serve another. Commuting home should have been some solace to him but being alone in a car was wasted if all he did was yell at everybody for not knowing how to drive. Multi-colored cars all around hissed poison in the atmosphere and with the air conditioner dead, the windows were doomed to stay down all summer. Before his choking worsened, the reprieve of his exit gave him the most satisfaction he had experienced all day. *Everyday*, Thomas thought to himself.

61

While cruising down the final stretch of his commute, a newly carved road through rows of tall pines, the air instantly improved in quality and scent. This final mile to the apartment complex was his path to Valhalla, always dying daily in battle to return to paradise. As was usual for sunny days, the sole sidewalk of the road was populated with people out to move their legs one final time before retiring. Darker skin and bright clothes were the usual common factor, Thomas noticed. Further down, almost to the end of the road, the contrasting and drably dressed young man he encountered earlier was among the few pedestrians just starting out on their evening walk.

Staring hard at the young man only further infuriated Thomas when he was not recognized in return. The insult collided with the previous insolent display to create an explosion of disgust, nearly forcing him to pull off onto the side of the road. Instead he finished the short drive home while devoting the remaining time to making up his mind. After he parked and got out of the car, his feet carried him left instead of forward in the direction of the door. Where the stretch of new road began was not very far from his apartment.

The tread of his long-legged gait was exceptional in how heavily each foot struck the pavement. With the gap between him and his solo objective shortening, his left hand involuntarily stiffened then formed a fist over and over, enough to capture Thomas' attention. He shrugged it off as nerves. The closer he got to his prey, the action's frequency increased to become an uncomfortable beacon. His left hand had become a permanent fist once he was less than forty feet away from the young man.

The target never even heard Thomas approach so the fist to the back of his head was a complete and utter surprise. Even if he did notice, he would have paid little attention to what would have been ignored like any other pedestrian. As the young man toppled forward from the blow, Thomas kicked his opponent's feet out from under him and helped him to the ground. More kicks followed, striking mostly the chest and head of the young man on the ground in too much pain to even cry out for help.

Lost in the exhilaration of adrenaline and animosity Thomas very quickly became so focused on furiously kicking the young man that he was in turn oblivious to anything but the task at hand. Then, unexpectedly, he too was taken off guard by a blow to the back of his head. It was not enough to knock him out cold, but it was enough to make him enraged. Spinning around with his fist ready to connect, he was again taken off guard by a body blow from another direction. This attack negated any violent response of his own and sent him to his knees, panting. Barely inhaling, another blow struck the side of his head. A foot to the face. One after another, kicks were administered along with weak punches to the head. They still stunned him and added to the stars he would see after every successive strike. Just as he was about to lose consciousness, a horn kept him from blacking out and the presence of an approaching vehicle scattered his assailants. His first breath afterwards was painful but satisfying

Happy Hour at Valentine's

After another soul crushing week, all I could think about was happy hour at Valentine's, a bar around the corner from the office. Their food is terrible but the drinks are strong, especially if you're a regular. When my group of friends roll in, at least one of the bartenders would yell, "Norm!" This was mostly directed at me. As with any standard Friday happy hour, one by one my co-workers would drop off; heading away to other dates or their children. I am blessed with neither but cursed by being alone. I'm not the most popular guy at work, anyway. I am liked enough to be invited but only tolerable for an hour and some change. I guess the same must be true outside of work, too.

Thankfully I've always been a happy drunk so the bartenders have only cut me off twice. Both times were when I had more beers than I was able to keep track of. And both times I showed my ID to prove that I lived within stumbling distance of the bar just down U Street, but still I was told no. The last time I went even further out of my way to show them the restriction on my license because I am almost legally blind and not technically supposed to drive a car, but all the bartender did was laugh. This then made me laugh.

With no one or nothing else waiting for me at home, I am the last man drinking from my group. I'm not on anyone's radar at work, being barely noticeable in my sizeable department. At work my productivity is kept slightly above average and always just enough to get by. Unpopular isn't the best word to describe me at work. More like discounted. This is what happens to people like me; you get out what you put in. Like I said earlier, a dozen of us from work go to happy hour then groups and singles leave like clockwork, making me feel as alone then as I am while everybody is talking around me to each other. I collect a couple of handout goodbyes thrown at me as a professional courtesy. The upside is that Alex usually gives me a beer on the house when the last of my crew leaves. He's become the other norm during Friday evening happy hours; our time at the bar beginning the same month. We never share much more than small talk. I believe we recognize some shared anti-social tendencies. This was confirmed one evening early on when we noticed each other mouthing the lyrics to the same song by the Smiths.

How is it I like happy hour, not to mention the once a week after work camaraderie of my co-workers if I'm socially anxious? I'm willing to put up with people I like for a few hours during my personal time in case there's a possibility of meeting a woman. Bars have always been comfortable to me and being out by myself has never been a problem. I'm not getting any younger. There haven't been many prospects so I put myself out there, or here, at Valentine's, every Friday evening in particular. This is the extent of my social activity, outside of work.

A stool at the far end of the bar is my favorite place to sit. From there I have a view of the room's entire square footage. It's a pretty small space compared to other bars in the area. With a direct view of the door that's down a short hallway, I can see who's coming in before the bartender. I like to believe it gives me the first pick of whatever single lady comes in for a drink, once she's close enough for me to determine whether or not

I'd be interested. All the pretty ones end up meeting a friend or I guess they are *too* pretty and out of my league. A lot of young professionals who work and live nearby also come here so an older guy like me barely gets a single glance. But its nice to look, anyway. It's harmless. I don't leer or make anybody feel uncomfortable. My thick glasses give me the protection of pity. This is why I like to sit at the end of the bar, away from most everybody else.

Cold beer washes away the week's worth of dirt and grime covering my insides. It can also wash away these silly, unfulfilled longings for a girlfriend and clear the way for me to think about normal things: groceries, news stories, possible weekend plans. Lately though I've been thinking about nothing, really, at all. A clear mind. Or numbed, probably. But not tonight. Non-stop whizzing thoughts in my head. Little things can't be bothered with. I am again thinking about what it would be like to have a girlfriend.

Loneliness is getting to me. It would be nice to have somebody granting me a little time with my co-workers before I had to meet her for dinner, or more drinks with *our* friends. A beautiful woman on my arm when I walk into a room isn't asking a lot. She doesn't have to have model looks; guys like me don't get women like that. I would be happy with almost anyone that showed even a slight interest and talked to me longer than two minutes. My standards aren't very high. I'm beginning to believe that the standards of the average lady in the bar are too high for me to see, let alone reach. Maybe I should look for another bar.

A throbbing bass line is barely audible under louder than usual chatter. Alex brings me another beer, seeing I am a sip away from killing the bottle I'm drinking. My head is pulsing from the quick gulp making me accidentally slam the bottle down. A simple misjudgment of the distance between the bottle and the wooden top of the bar.

"I asked if this seat is taken? The voice cut through the noise of the crowd and the humming in my head. Turning around almost makes me fall off the stool.

"No, I don't think so." My response is honest since I was so internalized. I have no idea. Immediately I wish I didn't say that. The response should've been more assertive, more informed. But there's no second chance for a first impression so I swivel back towards the bar and my beer. Her voice is soft and hypnotic when she orders, making it easy for me to fall back inside my thoughts.

Replaying the whole incident in my head is customary. Each run through is a little different than the last as I change it and mold it into the perfect interaction; maybe the reconstruction will be able to stand on its own and get me further than nervous small talk. Or maybe it will be part of a composite and an even more successful shot at an actual date. I get so lost in perfecting the past that I never notice her pay for the drink and leave right before another lady takes her place.

It is shocking to see another face staring at me from my left. My beer is empty and I don't want another. This time I am sure to pay attention when putting the bottle down. I look back at the lady and am stunned to see she is still looking back at me and smiling. Am I seeing all of this correctly?

Gone is the fake blonde hair of the previous sitter. Dark brown hair frames a beautifully round face which I find more welcoming than the sharp angles of the fake first lady. All I can do is stare dumbly until my brain shoots me a reminder to smile. Then I remember I've seen her here at Valentine's before. And I liked seeing her all those other times and I really like seeing her now. She seems more inviting and approachable since we're closer than before and both smiling at each other. Being so near, I fully see exactly how beautiful she is.

She has more confidence in her smile than I do, which I regret. As an older guy I should have more assurance since I interact with younger people all day but my experience with women is minimal. Alcohol always played a huge role whenever I've been able to take a lady home from the bar. Maybe this is going to be the case tonight. Here's hoping. The certainty of her smile and body language is contagious and my desire to seem more forward prompts me to speak first.

"What are you drinking?"

"Nothing yet. I just got here."

"Then what would you like?"

Her hand touches my knee as she leans in to tell me. The pressure of the contact is exciting. She senses this when my posture straightens, so her other hand gently cups the back of my head to bring me closer to her lips.

"Rum and coke please, handsome."

Her breathing is slow and warming to my ear. This adds to my stimulation. Squirming in my chair trying to discreetly shift and manage my visibly increasing stiffness isn't easy so I give up. It is dim enough, my pants are dark enough and even I have to really look, even with my poor eyesight, in order to tell.

"So, what's your name? Mine's Jenni with an 'I'."

"Mine is James."

"Nice to meet you, James."

We simultaneously begin to mention that we have noticed each other in the bar during other Friday happy hours then both stop and smile wider in awkwardness. This blushing makes her seem more human and does wonders to boost my present self-esteem.

"I come here every Friday after work with colleagues and end up staying when everyone else leaves."

"You don't have anybody waiting for you at home?"

"Nope. You?"

"Not anymore. I found out he's been fucking another girl so I guess that's that. Sorry to be so blunt. I guess I'm still a little pissed."

I sympathize genuinely.

Alex brings Jenni her drink and her swallows are more like large doses of medicine. Her cocktail is finished within sixty seconds. Before I can turn around and order her another, Alex replaces the empty glass with a freshly made rum and coke. The sign of a great bartender, I say to myself.

We talk and drink for nearly an hour. Not until she remarks that the bar isn't nearly as crowded as it was before are either of us fully aware of the dip in people. Valentine's is a dive bar, a place to go for cheap drinks before ending up at another, more popular bar or nightclub with unreasonable alcohol prices. The busiest I've ever seen it was when there were about thirty people to pack Valentine's to capacity. I've also been one of only three people in the bar. There are seven total that I presently counted, Alex included.

A glance at my watch earns me a jabbing reproach from Jenni, who reminds me that I previously mentioned not having anybody waiting on me. This is a nervous habit, I try and explain, but she puts her finger to my lips insisting I don't need to be nervous. What I need is to get up and use the bathroom but her hand is again on my knee.

I learn where she is from originally (Cleveland), what she does for a living (bank teller) and even where she lives (two and a half blocks from my building). I enjoy watching her mouth as she talks. When she realizes I am doing this she tensely asks if something is stuck in her teeth or something like that and I laugh. I tell her no but then I can't follow up with anything else. Her fingers tenderly reach out and lightly touch my face. Her compliment on how soft my beard is increases the sensation from her other hand that is now a bit past my knee and on my thigh. A melody can be detected in her voice, I swear.

I excuse myself when my squirming becomes impossible to manage. The reason is too many beers and not nerves, I promise her. My coat on the back of the high bar chair isn't enough of a guarantee that I won't cut and run. Just so she knows I'll come back and not leave her with the tab, I give Alex my credit card as insurance. I'm *joking,* she whispers while I get up, then again, she touches my face and beard with longer caresses. It feels so good and her words are so comforting that I almost lose my balance and fall. I probably would've pissed myself if I did fall.

It's hard and painful to piss with an erection and even harder to have much control with the limited space of a bathroom stall. I try the best I can and even attempt to wipe up as much as I can stand. While washing my hands I lean forward to get a better look at my face in the mirror. Too much alcohol makes me look red and splotchy but I'm doing good here, despite being pretty drunk. The cool water feels nice on my skin. Splashing water on my face isn't necessary, just customary. I'm not tired. It isn't an act of melodrama, the "I must be dreaming" response. The feeling is pleasant so I do it again.

The atmosphere of the bar changed during the ten minutes I spent in the bathroom. The same people are still there but less animated and talkative while staring at the new person talking to Jenni. His voice is loud enough to be heard over the music, this time a song by the Cure. This guy is yelling questions at her, never giving her enough time to answer before another one is shouted. Nobody notices me come out of the bathroom since all eyes are on this guy screaming his fool head off.

The bathrooms are at the opposite end of where I was sitting but I can still make out most of what he is saying. The questioning seems to be over.

"I can't believe you...this is where you go...I thought I had another chance..."

And so on. I stand there motionless, unsure of exactly what to do. I've never had to physically interfere with a boy/girl fight, or any fight for that matter. The possibility never presented itself until now. From the looks of it, I'd say the same is also true for everybody there. Except maybe Alex. He looks like he could kick an ass or two if necessary. So in the meantime I just follow suit and watch.

From where Jenni is sitting she has a clear view of me and where I am standing. Her glance never looks at anything other than her empty glass or anyone other than the guy. Two other people are at the bar, not far enough away to ignore it. They can hear everything better than anybody else while they stared and listened.

Is he going to hit her? He's getting closer and closer to her face and his hands fly around wildly when he speaks. His speech gets quiet once he becomes more aware that we are looking at the two of them, secretly or not. The volume drops lower but he can still be heard. Not once does he touch her, not even a hand on her shoulder or a grab of her arm. Would anybody do anything if he did hit her? Would I? Alex maybe would but probably only if the bar or its property are threatened. And since the guy has yet to lay a finger on her he doesn't have much reason to worry.

Over his voice I hear somebody ask the person they were with a question about their weekend plans. Those two are closer to me than Jenni and the guy so for a second I am engrossed in finding out the answer before the guy yells a little again which brings my attention back to him and Jenni. I never hear the response about weekend plans as I try to eavesdrop more on what he begins aggressively whispering to Jenni. At least two other people lose interest in the couple arguing. The rest of us are still paying attention however we are comfortable doing it. Those of us farther away and still paying attention now all openly stare.

"When is this going to end?" I think those words came from the guy but they didn't line up how his lips moved. Confused, I look around and see that a table of three has begun talking to each other since they quit paying attention. I then think this is a complaint about the argument but the two of them are more quiet than before. The guy with Jenni is still very animated and every so often a complaint of his own rises above the growing number of people all losing interest and carrying on with their own uninteresting conversations. Throughout it all, Jenni and the guy never look away from each other's space.

I notice I am the only person besides Alex not in a conversation. Staring at Jenni and the guy is proving unsuccessful at helping me hear what they're now talking about. I am still the farthest away and everybody is deliberately talking louder to avoid having anything else to do with the couple and their argument. My interests are easily led from one conversation to the next, depending on which is the loudest. The normal things everybody's talking about make me start thinking about them, too: groceries, news stories, possible weekend plans.

My head starts to hurt and I am tired of standing still. This is becoming more difficult as the drunkenness increases. It feels like thousands of pins started poking my left leg all at once. On instinct I shift more weight to my right leg but the reflex keeps me moving forward in the direction of Jenni and the guy. When I am a few yards from where they are, all of the attention turns to me since I am the only person to move a lot since the guy came in and started yelling about how they didn't break up because he didn't break up with her.

The guy turns around and looks right at me when he notices me heading in their direction. A visible tension tightens his body and straightens his posture. My body responds the same way after seeing his reaction. The closer I get, the better I can see him. Whether or not I can actually kick his ass doesn't matter. I'm not impressed. Tall and wiry with ugly white boy dread locks is all I need to see. Jenni keeps her eyes fixed on the empty glass between her hands. She wants to look at me, I can tell, but she doesn't.

"Hey! I asked you if there was a problem!" His voice lifts above everybody's gossip and work week complaints. Again, all eyes are on them, on us. More tension stiffens our bodies. Anticipation takes a hold of everybody. We all want to know what is going to happen next. Even Alex pays more attention.

The stand off doesn't last long at all but given the pressure it seems like forever. My response is surprisingly quick since I am only a little worried but my attention and interest in any further interaction with him or Jenni is gone.

"I just need to grab my jacket and credit card."

His body jerks when he realizes that Jenni must've previously been talking to me. Jenni flinches and tightens her hands around the glass. She still never looks at me. Always reactionary, my body answers by also hardening, but with my face twisting into an

82

uninterested surrender. I just want to get my stuff and go home. Moving the remaining distance to grab the jacket from the chair and then the card from Alex is nerve racking. Everybody is staring, again hoping for or expecting something physical, finally, from our corner.

What if I did just punch him in the face? I'd shock myself more than anybody else here. I had it in me and the thought does cross my mind. There is enough frustration from life, anger caused by other people and situations that I know wants to lash out but is it worth it? Is he? Is Jenni? Are the consequences of a broken nose or black eye or jail worth any of it? Not at all. Nothing is really worth anything.

Turning my back on them, the whole situation feels relieved. The thought that he might sucker punch me isn't much of a threat. I could see the same panic and anxiety in his eyes during our face-off. Deep down I know none of this, not even pretty Jenni, is really going to be worth a fight to either of us. To be young and stupid again, I think for a moment. Pushing open the door and stepping out into the chilly night I laugh while putting on my jacket. My body is shivering and at first I blame it on the drop in temperature. But my jacket and its warmth around me confirms I am shuddering at the thought of being young again. To get my mind off the subject I start thinking about how it is definitely time to find another bar.

Goldenrain Bridge

The autumn leaves were remarkably red. After a cold week's worth of rain, their yellowing was skipped over, turning to various oranges before finally burning a deep red. Against a sunlit sky they added fire to the heavens and heat to whatever found itself underneath their canopy. It was the start of the Indian summer and an appreciated reprieve from the gloom of perpetual rain.

Underneath the thickest shelter of trees that stretched an entire block was one of three crosswalks; two parallel white lines intersecting Becontree Lane just before Goldenrain Court and its residential neighborhood across from the elementary school. To the older kids it was ignored – crossing the street wherever they wanted became a sign of rebellion. They were not babies in need of the assistance of guards or imaginary boundaries or permission. To the younger children who attended the elementary school, it was the only way to cross Becontree Lane. The importance of using it to safely cross the street was instilled in them on the first day of school and even more so by those living in the vicinity of the crosswalk the kids named the Goldenrain Bridge.

The younger children were thankful but confused by the false start to fall while the parents found relief that it kept their houses empty for a few extra hours after school. Usual pockets of play formed around the neighborhood according to age and grade. The basketball court and the surrounding concrete area by the elementary school: parking lots, sidewalks and the outdoor athletic area became the territory of lazy, loitering older middle school kids who went to the larger school a few blocks away. Directly across the street were more wooded and natural areas of the neighborhoods. These spaces became magnets for the budding imaginings of the younger children. Every day that week after school the weather grew more agreeable and easily enough, any questions about the flashback to summer were abandoned. "Better enjoy it while it lasts," flew from most grownups' lips.

The warmth and unobstructed sunshine continued into the weekend. Saturday was greeted by early risers still eager and grateful to be outside. Many kids were up before their hungover or otherwise exhausted parents. More denizens populated the

87

outdoors and made their appropriate divisions as the temperature rose alongside the trajectory of the yellow fireball in the sky. Before noon it was already approaching eighty degrees.

"There is no way in hell you kissed a girl, you lying sack of shit!" Saving face before that accusation would be difficult but with no one around knowing differently, Lewis went with his invention.

"Hell yeah I did," Lewis loudly retaliated, "she even let me grab her boob." Nobody's expression changed to show belief in what was said. Further disappointment followed as Lewis realized he would not have been able to convince even himself if he were among the crowd. But he could think quicker than most, and this often served him well. "Y'all think it's bullshit?" Lewis proclaimed more than asked with amplified bravado. "She was my grandma's neighbor and one night, after everybody was asleep, we snuck out and met up. We talked for a little bit but all she really wanted to do was kiss. I felt her boob and she didn't complain so I figured why stop there? But before I could start going to third base, my grandma woke up and I had to sneak back inside before I got caught."

A few more of the assembly became enthralled and he could tell the tale was gaining Lewis favor. Fake or not, most just wanted to hear a good sex story so he set out to astound. Momentum was needed for his story to sound authentic. "I'll tell you what-" Lewis began, but his words were cut short by a hard, open-handed pat in the middle of his back. The wind needed to finish his sentence was knocked out by the force of the blow. A deep intake of air was painful but necessary before Lewis could turn around and face his assailant.

"You'll tell us what?" Ed asked. Lewis was still trying to catch his breath. "That's what I thought," Ed continued, "you were gonna tell us some bullshit about how you got lucky but you're so full of shit you're choking on it." Everyone's attention went to Ed while he addressed the crowd with banter meant for Lewis. "Remind us again, you did what at your grandma's house before she almost caught you?"

The masses swelled and pushing her way to the front was Linda. To Lewis' horror, his sister answered. "We were staying up late watching *The Exorcist* and when my grandma got up we had to pretend we were asleep so she wouldn't get mad." Silence fell after Linda spoke and flitted off toward the street. All eyes were on her as she momentarily paused at one end of the Goldenrain Bridge, looked both ways two times then crossed precisely in the middle of the parallel lines. With one sudden snap, all eyes again fell on Lewis, whose face was red with anger and embarrassment.

Ed was quick to speak. "So, does that mean you were making out with your little sister?" Audible gasps and chuckles escaped a couple of mouths. Lewis was frozen in fear. "No defense?" Ed asked. "Didn't you say you felt her up, too? She doesn't even have tits!" Ed howled with laughter and most of the swarm joined, either willingly or uncomfortably. Lewis merely stood there, slightly trembling and only able to take in brief, sharp breaths. "Sad," Ed commented as he patted a flinching Lewis on the shoulder, first soft then successively harder until he made Lewis wince, "really fucking sad. No wonder you've never had a girlfriend, you've got the hots for your sister, you pervert." Walking away, Ed became a magnet attracting his simple herd away from that day's pariah, whose face was nearly as red as the few leaves from the branches overhead that were landing at his feet.

The rest of the day gave Lewis all the time he might need to gather and harness all his anger and concentrate that rage at his younger sister, the unknowing ruiner of reputations. Would he be able to show his face at school on Monday? What consequences were waiting for him when he rejoined the ranks of his classmates? Lewis felt this to be the worst possible thing and that his life was over at the early age of fourteen. Just like the other boys his age, sex was terrifying and always on their minds. Impulses were forced down their throats and they came from any place possible, secular or sanctified. But unlike most other boys his age, his anxieties came from suppressing unfamiliar impulses towards those other boys. Lying about sex was a safety valve if the pent-up steam wasn't released by actual sex. The falsehood might have been believed if his sister

91

didn't come along at the most inopportune moment. Ed the bully was also to blame, but Lewis knew he couldn't deal with Ed. Linda, on the other hand...

All through dinner Lewis could hardly hide an annoyed disposition. Since he refused to say anything about what was bothering him, it was easily written off by everyone at the table as perpetual teen angst. Even Linda offered no insight as to why Lewis might be acting in such a way. Right in front of him they asked his sister as if he were in another room. All she did was shrug her shoulders, by then beyond indifferent. Another typical Saturday supper, the adults agreed with nods.

An urgency to be the first one up and away from the table was usual for Lewis. Laying on his floor and staring at the ceiling in silence, he waited for Linda to finish and return to her room. She did sooner than he expected, the reason quickly gleaned through paper-thin walls. Giggling more than ever was a good indication that she was on the phone and probably talking about some cartoon or joke that was funny only to little kids.

Lewis made the decision to stay on the floor and block out his sister's childish back and forth over the phone.

Before too long, Lewis became aware that the room next to his was silent. Its occupancy was confirmed when he heard Linda's bed creek. Lewis slowly picked himself off the cool floor and left his room on tip-toes. Pausing when he reached her door, Lewis inhaled quietly and deep. With a sudden explosion of movement, he threw open the door and emptied his lungs with a shout. She was embarrassingly startled into throwing the pillow she had on top of her and between her legs.

What his sister was doing was initially lost on Lewis. His delight came from both scaring her and the outcome. This was only the beginning of his planned harassment. Still at the door, Lewis was amused at Linda's discombobulation and still didn't notice her face flush with embarrassment. Assuming it was anger he quickly tried to think what he should do next to keep her annoyance rising.

Satisfaction would have been his regardless of what resulted from his first offense. More violence would have been preferred but he would rile her up to that point. He was one of a very select few who could crack Linda's peaceful shell. Taunting more than asking, Lewis requested to know what his little sister was up to and why she had a pillow on top of her instead of underneath. In the middle of asking, the answer became known but he continued. This would get under her skin enough to bring about more of the consequences he wanted. But this didn't work as expected; the little upturn of inflection at the end of his jabbing question only flipped the switch that activated distress.

Her attempt at any excuse would have made Lewis laugh, more from her fumbling after a plausible reason. Any time she endeavored to speak, the short effort would be interrupted by a terrible stuttering. Tears welled after her failure at a fourth and final time so Lewis abruptly changed his approach and revealed his plan to her. "I'm just messin'..." Lewis kept repeating until Linda's tears dried. "Hell, sometimes I do it too," he admitted, slyly, "because sometimes it's just more comfortable that way. Why do you think I have so many pillows?"

Laughter erupted from both siblings. A solidarity was achieved, the opposite of what Lewis first expected to do. The corners of his mouth remained creased, insisting that the sentiment was genuine. Any cold-hearted plans for revenge evaporated. Without knowing for sure or why, both believed they were on equal footing for once. This was also unpredicted by Lewis but completely appreciated by Linda. She smiled at being in on a joke with her brother rather than being the butt of an insult or wise crack.

"Wanna know what Tallara and I were talking about and why we were laughing?" Linda was desperate to change the subject and Lewis politely accepted. "Well, she heard at school today that Mary is pregnant...and its Ray's!"

Lewis raised his eyebrows in mock surprise to encourage further revelations. Linda took the bait and kept going.

"Anabelle saw them at recess, behind the cafeteria, and they kissed FOREVER! Everybody knows that if you kiss longer than five seconds and you're not

wearing a raincoat then you'll probably get pregnant."
Reactionary as always, Lewis busted out laughing.

"Really? So, you're telling me that Mary is
pregnant?" With eyes wider than saucers, Linda's head
shook slowly up and down.

Through clenched teeth, Lewis asked whether
anybody else knew about it. "Only everyone in school!"
Linda confirmed. Thankfully by then, Lewis was able to
subdue his laughter and loosened his tight jaw to speak
more clearly. His question was meant to further prod
and make his little sister continue her juvenile
explanation of how biology worked. It was difficult to sit
through the stories without telling her how misinformed
she was, but for a change Linda was amusing him and
not being a pest.

Listening intently, Lewis reacted whenever
necessary with whatever successfully kept Linda talking
about anybody. From her supposedly pregnant
classmate she went on into the personal lives of most all
the students at Forest Edge Elementary School. He
knew just from listening to her talk tirelessly about other

people that she was doomed to become the type of girl he

hated: always in people's business and not able to keep

her mouth shut about any of it. She would ruin more

reputations, break up relationships and perpetuate

rumors all the while thinking she was doing nothing

wrong. That malicious stage had not been reached. The

sheen of innocence still coated the words that revealed

so many personal lives. To Linda, she was only relaying

information to anybody interested. Lewis was in awe of

his sister's purity and naiveté but worried about the

invading influence of humanity.

When the subject turned to boys, Linda became

noticeably energized. Extra sucking of teeth punctuated

sentences about boys on sports teams or a hunky male

coach or teacher. Ears perked up when she conferred

about a boy named Adam, Ed's little brother. Lewis

observed the exceptional agitation that animated her

limbs and eyes while on the topic. Offensive teeth

sucking was replaced by veritable sighs. Lewis was quick

to interrupt with a question. "Do you like Adam?" he

demanded to know. Impressed as he was at keeping the

97

playful smile slapped on his face, he allowed the strain to goad an even larger, interested smile.

"Maybe," Linda answered with her glance cast at her feet dangling off the side of the bed.

"Can you tell me why?" This opened her eyes wider than her mouth as the list of reasons poured forth. Any physical attributes described were similar to Ed's, just exaggerated on the adolescent older brother. These likenesses were noted as reasons why Lewis and most everybody else envied Ed. The legitimate attentiveness was observed and she seized the random opportunity to have an authentic conversation with her brother like when they were both younger.

"He's only the cutest guy in the third grade!" Her tone was incredulous; after all, *everybody* knew that. If what Linda mentioned of his personality and behavior were true then Adam was very much the opposite of his brother: good grades, pitcher on the baseball team and allowed a better disposition. Lust was almost fully awake and burning in Linda's eyes like beacons for experience.

To Lewis, they were the embers of an exhausted childhood.

The desire to hate Adam because of his brother was logical but unjustifiable. Opinions about his sister's attraction to the brother of his enemy devolved into more hostile sentiments towards Ed. Knowing just how to use this knowledge as a knife to fillet off a layer of skin would be advantageous for the bully. Lewis did not want him to have any more leverage than he already controlled. His listening became more focused once he realized his sister was in the middle of a monologue about Adam that might be used against his big brother.

Another name began to pop up more often and from what Lewis could tell it must have been Adam's best friend. What he could also tell was that Adam must be gay. He and his best friend Philip were practically inseparable. They dressed alike, talked alike and tolerated few besides each other. During baseball practices, Philip sat in the bleachers until Adam was done and off they would walk home, Philip carrying both of their books and listening dutifully about the mechanics of baseball.

Polite attention provided further proof, according to Lewis. With each reveal about Adam, he scolded himself for not having known any of this sooner. How did his sister not see the truth, either? Did anybody else in the third grade? Nevertheless, Lewis had ammunition. Ed's style was to find a victim and haunt them relentlessly until violence erupted. It was a matter of fact that he would be waiting for Lewis Monday to further his torment. A strange readiness became present, surely from the armament of his newfound information.

Sunday came and went; thunderstorms gathered later in the evening, lit up the sky and rumbled the ground. Over Monday's breakfast it was learned that nobody slept very well, or at all, in Lewis' case. A silence suppressed what was usually a more dynamic time of day. There was no sense of urgency or purpose in the actions of the parents. The children followed their example. Everything from getting up, getting ready and getting out the door was delayed thirty minutes. The parents could be late for work and they knew a note sent with their children would be enough to excuse their tardiness. Panic was not a priority since coffee barely did the trick.

At last, clothes were hastily selected and thrown over the kids' sluggish bodies before they were ushered out the door and down the street towards their schools. Youthful exuberance propelled Linda further ahead than Lewis, who lagged behind with his face aimed up at the sky. The overnight rainclouds were still heavy in the sky; a menacing presence looked as though more storms may come. The break in the east where the sun peaked over the horizon offered optimism. The heavens were a chromatic shift moving upward from gray to pink, then to deep purple where swaths of gold and blue began to cut their way past the remaining dreariness.

A wet mat of leaves covered most of the ground, making it hard to differentiate sidewalks from front yards. Lewis shuffled his feet and kicked the red foliage to clear his own path. For a few seconds it all made him feel contented and gave him a sense of cordiality with the last thawing rays of the Indian summer. A beat later it all came rushing out of him; this orientation and connection to his environment, along with all the air filling his lungs. His stomach burned as he fell to the ground near a football. The missile, Lewis reckoned.

The noise in his ears subsided, clearing the way for the laughter that rang through and wracked his brain. A connective hurt ran from his head down to his cramped stomach. A couple harsh intakes of air caused the ache to worsen but they were worth the relief of controlled breathing. The laughter came nearer and closed in around Lewis. Picking himself up was useless; each attempt was met with a foot that swept whichever hand or leg tried to give him leverage from being flat on the ground. Ed was the individual assailant, the others had gathered merely as spectators.

"Get up!" Ed finally shouted his permission. Unsure of whether it was a trick, Lewis hesitated. A hand grabbed him by the collar of his shirt and helped him to his feet. Blood rushed from his head to make him dizzy again and unsteady. Noticing, Ed again swept

Lewis' legs out from under him. The laughter resumed, and taunting began to come from the mouths of others, not just Ed's. His was just the loudest as he came rushing upon the still strewn body of his opponent. "Get the fuck up!" The command came in a staccato intonation along with another accompanying hand ripping Lewis off the ground.

All the previous disorientation resumed, bringing with it extra disruption from a cacophony of laughter. The mixed blessing of Ed's hand steadying him on his feet was not lost on Lewis. The pounding in his head was loud enough to have come from Ed's fists but there was no outside pain since no physical blows were dealt. Focus returned to Lewis moments before he was paraded counter clockwise around the circle that gathered to witness his humiliation.

"What did you do last night?" Ed wondered out loud. He had to ask a couple times before it registered to Lewis that a question was being posed. For every two times Ed had to ask, he issued a light, taunting slap across Lewis' face and said, "wake up."

Bewildered still and opening his mouth to answer, Lewis finally heard the words being spoken and they were not his own. Reeling his head toward the voice revealed that again his little sister was speaking in his place. Panic forced his attentions to dramatically focus on what she was saying. "We stayed up talking. Well, I did most of the talking. Lewis just listened mostly. He listens good."

"And what were y'all talking about? Lewis' imaginary girlfriend?" This drew an uproar from the cluster, most of whom witnessed Saturday's occurrence. It was time for Lewis to interrupt his sister before she had a chance to respond.

"We were mostly talking about your faggot brother." Lewis wrongly thought his remark would stun Ed and cause him to loosen the grip on his shirt. Lewis would be able to shimmy free and either run or punch Ed in the face, or both. What was said didn't sway the crowd's support to Lewis, nobody joined him in shaming Adam. Nothing turned out in Lewis's favor. First came an immediate blow from Ed's heavy fist to the center of his belly. Lewis threw up the meager contents of his breakfast, his bully abruptly released him with a powerful shove to the ground. Knees and hands slid in vomit as he fell. Slowly he lifted his head in anticipation of another blow that was not coming.

Looking around at the assembly, Lewis noted that all eyes were on him. Their passion changed from nosy to outraged. Whispers sounded quietly then became louder until everybody was murmuring something to somebody. Besides Lewis, the only person silent was Linda. She stared at him while tears ran from her eyes and down her face. It was obvious that his little sister was trying to make sense of her feelings and give them a voice, but she couldn't think of what to say. All she did was shake her head in frustration.

"I know my brother's gay! What's your fucking problem with that?" Ed's screaming question preceded another blow. Brick-like knuckles slammed into the side of his face and Lewis swiveled before landing flat on the ground, fully extended in his vomit. The powerful fist then held Lewis' shirt in a vice tight grip and lifted him up and back onto his feet in one swift motion. Just as promptly as he rose up he was knocked back to the ground with a fist and a warning. "NOBODY calls my brother a faggot!"

"STOP!" Linda shrieked, her voice cutting through the crowd to shatter their thoughts. One word ultimately gathered the force needed to manifest in her throat and become a command. The attention on Linda overwhelmed her too much at once. Trembling, unsure nerves informed her decision to fly instead of continuing any semblance of a fight. "I'm going to get mom and dad!" she declared before pivoting and dashing off towards home.

Enough damage was done to an already non-existent reputation and parental involvement would be the kiss of death. He was a year shy of high school and Lewis still held on to the hope that some sort of reinvention would be possible as he grew up and became a truer version of himself. Linda must not be allowed to reach the house only a few hundred yards away from his disgrace.

The diversion of Linda's outburst and fleeing still captivated the throng of people. The break was exactly what Lewis needed and when he recognized the opportunity to pursue his little sister, he went for it. Easily unimpeded by anybody else once he was free from Ed, Lewis advanced upon Linda. His focus wasn't on his tears or burning gut but was fixed on the objective of stopping his sister. Linda's focus was directed solely upon their house and a precipitous flash illuminated her brother's thoughts with the portending of something grave. Impending nearness to Linda brought with it further recognition of potential calamity.

The Goldenrain Bridge was more than thirty feet from where Lewis could almost reach his sister. Linda's concentration on her objective was so complete that she never heard her brother's heavy feet stomping up from behind. Even the shouting of her name couldn't disrupt the effort. A split second later and she was close enough to be grabbed. Reaching out suddenly with a jerking motion promised an advantage of several inches but instead upset the boy's balance. Rather than snatching her back towards the grass, his feet slid on the carpet of drenched leaves and he stumbled off the curb, knocking Linda into the street.

Hitting the ground hard and skidding his hands and knees on the road, Lewis yelled a profanity. The tiny protrusion on the top of his wrist and just below the surface of his skin confirmed a broken bone. His holler wasn't as loud as the screech of skidding tires. His spill into the street and fractured wrist were less compelling to the crowd as the scene that involved a little girl and a car.

Pushing himself up with his less damaged hand, Lewis hobbled over to the commotion, repeating his sister's name back and forth between a scream and a choked whisper. Seeing his little sister face down and motionless on the asphalt forced an audible gasp to only once replace the sounding of her name. His mouth still formed the word as it began to echo on the lips of the curious who followed behind at a respectful distance, still predictably interested in what might happen next.

Gingerbread Boy

The air outside was beginning to maintain the freshness that early April often promised. Alan's allergies so far were spared but as he walked from his apartment towards the barbershop, he could not help but wonder for how long. *Enjoy it while it lasts.* That became a daily affirmation when he turned seventy. The ideal time of the day to get his haircut was early enough that the busy town center traffic barely stirred. No crowds. No noise. More importantly, an appointment meant no wait.

The barber shop opened at nine so on the first Saturday of every month Alan was waiting for the door to be unlocked. Routine was a fearful gateway to stagnation and the last thing he wanted was to become an old man. All that was left of his hair circled his skull; there was some gray but a measure of red remained. He embraced aging and even the eventuality that ensued but he refused to waste away, decrepit and useless in the winter of life. Walks, a gym membership and yoga kept fears at bay. Exercise was less for vanity and more for preservation and perseverance.

A new face with a built-in smile opened the door. Alan returned the courtesy. Receptionists have come and gone in the past year and a half but the only face he wanted to see was standing behind his barber's chair with a genuine, glowing smile. Alan responded in kind; the forced pleasantry for the receptionist swelled into one of sincerity as he approached the waiting chair. The three things that made him happy at the first of the month were now all confirmed: retirement check direct deposited in the bank, the cleaning lady straightened up and deep cleaned until next payday and, at last, his appointment with Kevin.

Kevin's traditional black shop smock was over a white dress shirt fastened all the way to the top button. Black slacks descended from his waist to the tops of his shiny, patent leather shoes. Meticulous hair kept short crowned his head where gray only threatened to overtake his temples. Dark, unblemished skin offered no real distinction of nationality. A thick accent afforded no additional clues and Alan was too embarrassed to ask. With a flourishing hand gesture Kevin motioned him into the seat. Anybody in the chair was treated like royalty,

111

but Alan assumed his place as a monarch would a throne. With a wave of the black vinyl cape across his client's chest the finishing touch of accoutrement was in place for his highness.

"The same, Mr. Alan?"

"The same, Mr. Kevin."

Eyes closed with anticipation, Alan could run through the entire procedure of getting his hair cut and face shaved from memory. Instead he let his mind go blank, exhaled and waited. The faint twist of a small plastic lid made the hair on the back of his neck spark with electricity. It collected at the nape until Kevin lightly rubbed freshly mentholated fingers on Alan's scalp. A bolt of lightning shot to the tips of his toes and a million pin pricks stayed after the initial shock of contact. Mint soothed Alan whenever he noticed the smell. Peppermint from his grandmother when he was a kid, mint julips during adulthood; tense years of worrying and explicit hard times were made bearable from some minty remedy. Relieved nerves were the consequence. What would Kevin think if Alan requested a longer scalp massage? Every time he decided it would be inappropriate. After all, Kevin was a professional and who was Alan to appeal for more time than the appointment allotted?

A fresh cotton towel was draped across then tucked into the neck of the apron. Muscle memory took over and he leaned forward to support himself as Kevin reclined the back of the chair. When he heard the final click, Alan gently leaned back and placed his neck in the curved edge of the sink. The correct gauging of water temperature was a show Kevin's familiarity. The heat of the spray was comforting and relaxed Alan beyond the effects of the head massage. The extra attention to his scalp confused him since there was no hair on the top of his head. Wondering but never asking why was enough, as was the beam on Kevin's face during the routine. Rinsing with warm water was Alan's favorite part. Millions of small bubbles washed off his head and Alan swore he could feel every single one. Each bubble swirling down the drain took away more of a past he was hoping to outlive.

Anything that touched Alan's head or neck after the shampoo and rinse sent surges through his body. The worst visible reaction would be a twitching of his legs. The simple act of a plastic comb running through his hair was incomparable when the black teeth were under the command of Kevin's skilled hand. Each stroke was precise and before Alan could ever fully lose himself in the occurrence, it would end. Alan knew these motions were functional, not significant. Caution was always practiced to not get purposes confused; propriety was paramount and Alan did not ever want Kevin to get any wrong ideas. The cut always continued with a peaceful, satisfied smile spread across the barber's face.

Cold metal against his neck and the base of his skull created then amplified the most evocative sensations. Tactile recollections offered the strongest links to his past. And should any memory have a strong fragrance associated with it, Alan could unintentionally travel back in time. A barber shop was a vortex where all spirits, remembrances, smells and wants intersected and collided.

The click of an electric razor, seemingly unchanged since his youth, and the initial cold steel pressed against the back of his head made Alan shudder. Kevin learned to anticipate this reaction so after the first upward swipe with his clippers he would pause and his smile would broaden. Nostalgia for simpler times progressively eroded when Alan finally came to understand that those years were not uncomplicated at all, just made tolerable by family money and privilege. All of it would have been given up since it kept him tethered to his parents until the end of their senselessly long lives. Without their singular inspiration, would these episodes even exist to excite or upset him?

Gray hair dusted the shoulders of the cape. A closer look revealed a fair amount of dull red. It resembled a dusting of cinnamon and sugar, or a few dying embers smoldering among ashes. Years ago his hair was a vivid orange. In the bright day sun, he was the kid everybody pointed at and teased by saying his head was on fire. Daring bullies during those abysmal years poured water on his head, laughing while telling him they were only looking out for his safety. A source of shame during his formative years, he always wished he were blond. When in later years it started graying, Alan pined for the days of being called the gingerbread boy.

When he was a kid, Alan's father took him at the first of the month to get their hair cut. A stop at the barber was part of the Saturday circuit when the family lived in Richmond's Shockoe Bottom. The order was always the bank, pay bills, barber, malts, grocery then home. Everything was within walking distance and these monthly jaunts counted highest among the few favorable times with his father.

Tickling the back of his neck would be the first thing Alan did when his cut was finished. His father watched and humored him until Alan got older and then tried explaining that it made everybody look at him funny. "It's weird," was the end of the discussion. Alan took to going outside and sitting on the side of the building in the alley to tenderly run his fingers across his neck and head. This was mimicry of the barber's upward strokes. Ultimately the gestures were indistinguishable and Alan smiled while thinking about the handsome barber with a mustache. Prickly hair delighted his finger; he felt the regeneration begin and became transformed.

North winds heralded change and a particularly fierce gust froze his bare fingers one day. Still, Alan dutifully brushed the back of his neck and head. "Has anybody ever told you your hair makes it look like your head's on fire?" The voice surprised Alan by being softer and higher in register than the booming voice that regularly snatched him from the shameful habit. He quickly turned around to see a kid his own age staring wide eyed at his hair. Where Alan might resemble an alabaster statue, the young child opposite him was an ebony effigy of a youthful African deity. An exchange of fascination over their unusual coloring was initiated between the two.

"My name is Alan."

"So is mine! How do you spell yours?"

"A-L-A-N."

117

"I spell mine with two 'L's and an "E.""

"You know how to spell?"

"And read, if you can believe it." Allen's laughter stunned Alan, who never registered the jest. "A lot of us know how to read and write, we just still don't go to your schools."

They walked closer to each other, never once taking their eyes from the enchanting black skin and red hair. Face to face, instincts insisted a mutual and demonstrative respect of Alan's hair and Allen's skin. Nerves turned their actions shaky and regrettable. Awkward, mutual admiration continued until Allen was taken by a need to look *and* feel more of Alan's soft and freshly cut hair. Unsure hands reached out, seized Alan by the shoulders and spun him around.

Words were arranged to form an eventual question that was never asked. Colder fingers than his own rubbed the back of Alan's head, especially near the nape of his neck where the hair line expertly faded away into his skin. Infinitely better than unfeeling electric razors, charged fingers pleased as they caressed carefully cropped red hair. Heat burned behind Allen's touch. Alan welcomed the impression and wished his head were truly covered in flames. He closed his eyes while his sense of understanding became overpowered. So much confused Alan; what about a foreign hand performing a personal and familiar function made him feel different and exceptional?

"ALAN!"

Both boys flinched and turned towards the deep voice saying their name.

"Yes?" Their responses were in unison, perfect and identical in tone and duration. Angry faced, Alan's father balled up his fist tightly before extending his forefinger and pointing to his side. Obeying was immediate and involuntary. Innocently, Alan offered to explain away his father's confusion. "His name is Allen but spelled different from mine."

"Different than yours, son," Alan's father corrected. "And different *from* you."

Alan was whisked away too quickly to have a final look at Allen. The vague blur of a face was all he could remember by the end of that day. The imaginativeness of his fiery hair burning a boy's fingers, turning them black and ashen, began instantly.

Dark hands kindly grabbed his shoulders to spin Alan around and out of his daydream. Opening his eyes, he faced himself in a three-quarter length mirror. Kevin broke the silence.

"How do you like?"

The answer was affirmative: a nod and a smile. Hands smoothed away any excess hair left from the cut before the chair was turned forty-five degrees then tilted into a recline. A tender caress across a stubbled face was only the beginning of more marvels.

Contrasting and cool shaving cream was applied with customary upward strokes. A deep breath and final nervous swallow preceded Kevin's careful removal of stubble. Paternal threats once induced a hasty reaction that informed Alan of the potential danger from a naïve slip of the blade. The few times Alan thought he might ask Kevin to finish with an electric shaver, he would look through his squinted and myopic eyes. What looked like the same burned and ashen hands of an older Allen cradled his head. Accustomed sensitivities returned and matured the same sixty years as Alan. Years of anxiety and disgrace might eventually be reconciled but it would still take time. Possibly more time than Alan had left.

The shave was over before Alan completed any serious deliberation. Face inspected and wiped clean, Kevin raised the back of the chair upright and took a closer look to make sure nothing was missed or out of place. Appreciation for Kevin's attention to detail would be reflected in his tip.

"Now you are even more handsome than before," Kevin stated and hearing it always made Alan blush.

"Thank you," Alan said, "it's only because of you."

The most they carried on conversationally was when the next appointment was made for the first Saturday of the following month. Before Alan paid the cashier, a brand new twenty-dollar bill was presented to

Kevin. After a final goodbye to the barber, he exited and walked around the neighborhood a while before returning home.

The weather was improving and Alan wanted to be out in the sun. Traffic was still light and the pollen count low. The further away he walked from the barbershop, the more he allowed Kevin to recede from his mind. Thoughts of his barber were a distinctive moment for Alan, a link to a part of him that shame or pedigree kept buried for so long. Once a month was sufficient since it took so much out of him to get a thirty-minute cut and shave at the barbershop.

Rock Creek: A Pastoral

Living two miles from the epicenter of a useless and oppressive government but still well within what could potentially be ground zero can wear anybody down, but only if they let it happen. For fifteen years I've seen the power ebb and flow from weak blue tides to the present deadly red tide and miraculously I've only ever ruined a few good pairs of shoes and pants. Those of us who live here have our ways of sloughing off the grimy film from life in the District. The concert halls and theatres. Some of the best food is within a two-mile radius of Dupont Circle. The weekly protests. All the shopping from cheap knockoff bags to their designer originals and everything in between lines nearly every major street. And in certain areas, plentiful trees and parks are available for respites with cleaner breathing and shade.

Walks down Connecticut Street to and from work five times a week is good for the body but terrible for the lungs since too many cars choke a city with limited streets but adequate public transportation. Only a few trees sparsely populate the southeast course to my office near Farragut Square and the northwest return home. I feel sorry for these prisoners and their life of constant mockery by the unnatural concrete that both towers and surrounds them. Church Street between 18th and 17th, where I live, offers more gracious shade from trees taller than my house. But even they long for more than an occasional wave from their neighbors to the west, those belonging to the urban forest of Rock Creek Park.

It is a brisk fifteen-minute walk from home; through the circle to continue onto P Street then I can be swallowed by a concentrated but limited canopy of leaves and branches. True, Rock Creek Parkway runs nearby and pollutes the air with more than its noise, but marginally fresher air and immersion in nature is the true solace offered further northwest along the trail, where the taller trees are allowed to grow, helping to lessen the noise. A few days a week I'll jog several miles along that route to clear my head and focus on the cadence of my feet pounding along the path. Jogging days haven't settled into anything resembling a habit. Only on Fridays, after a long week of bureaucratic bullshit and battered breathing, is a ritual refresh taken in the form of an hour walk around the park between P Street and M Street.

Dusk is perfect; late enough that the street traffic decreases in accord with the sunlight streaking the sky. Air quality is better and with this comes an improved visibility in spite of the dusk to navigate the snaking path along the rocky creek. Deep intakes of noticeably cleaner air clear away the angry smoke of the daytime city. Profuse oxygen always intoxicates me at first, enough to slow my pace along the trail. Communing with nature is essential for me to recharge and I steady my equilibrium with the sounds, smells and feel of nature. The crunch of sand and loose gravel as it shifts under my feet fills my head, the scent of wet leaves opens my brain to extrasensory altitudes. My footsteps become louder and louder only to fall out of sync with each other, a tell-tale sign of being trailed.

When my heightened senses tumble back to earth, I remember the ritual. The out of sync and heavy footsteps close in slow and my heart races. Another nature lover, I expect. Another person like me taking physical refuge in momentary breaks from a city hellbent on glorifying its own hubris. But how alike is he? Is his return to nature a recreational form of protest like it is for me? How much so? Eye contact is the best way to determine intention and either way a polite smile does wonders. The courteous and furtive grin returned often mirrors mine as the other person approaches. A simultaneous, downward gesture is made to pronounce and display the excitement at meeting a similarly inclined fellow. Roles are assumed and a congress obscene only in its efficiency is formed then dismissed...miraculous evidence that common ground can make anybody come together. Breath mingles in goodbyes and we go along our separate ways, him to wherever and me back home.

People find consolation in nature; its promise to renew and nurture is alluring and proven. The way it calls out to me might be peculiar compared to someone else's conversation – but it is the same call, on the same line, from the same operator. My instructions are no more unnatural than the next person's, they just tend to infuriate the people who don't listen to what their own spirit is trying to tell them. Like the men ruling from their big white houses and buildings down the street. And if it's an affront to their stagnant sensibilities then I'm glad I'm doing it, out in the open, right in their own backyards.

Kiss Me Like You Kissed Lizzie

July evenings were notoriously sloppy and difficult to manage. Virginia became wetter every year around the seventh month and Bernadette was aware that it rained on the same day for the past thirty years. *On her day.* July 21st. Everyone said rain on your wedding day was good luck but she thought the opposite and knew that old wives' tale to be untrue. Every year was another turn around the downward spiral to a mundane but well maintained grave. Everything she ever wanted weighed her down and threatened to hasten her being compacted and interred underground.

Thirty years, Bernadette thought as Ben drove through the pouring rain. Sure, she had whatever her heart desired but the older she became the less substantial her requests for tangible objects. By the arrival of their twentieth anniversary she no longer received joy from material things. If Bernadette at thirty had lost interest in gifts and baubles then Bernadette at fifty came to crave only attention. Her husband only had so little to spare and barely gave her any. Under the guise of work Ben would come home late in the evening and some months he would be gone for a couple days at a time. In those often long thirty years, Ben worked hard so that his wife wouldn't have to, so she could help the nanny raise the kids if she wanted or do nothing at all but eat and get fat if that's what her heart desired. But what she desired from her husband incessantly since the first time they met was passion. Ben only seemed to find delight in his lucrative vocation.

Lightning flashed across the sky behind the rooftops lining 9th Street. "A few more blocks to the restaurant," Ben said aloud as the car crossed I Street. The effect of the buildings against the lightning reminded him of the murder mystery movies his mother liked to watch. In a way, Bernadette reminded him of his mother, a fact that facilitated his falling in love. His thoughts remained singular and calm as he pulled up to the valet.

Throughout dinner, Bernadette watched her husband and noticed that he did everything methodically and with little feeling. This behavior was common but often ignored, which was her standard reaction to such passivity. When the valet complimented the sportscar he felt fortunate enough to park, Ben barely reacted. When asked about his food, his reaction was a brief nod. "When will he wake up?" Bernadette wondered, but with thirty years under their belt she finally accepted the correct answer to that question. "Another bottle of wine," she commanded, "and as soon as possible." There was no reaction from Ben.

"Doesn't our waitress look like Lizzie?" Ben asked as Bernadette finished off a glass of wine.

Her response was a direct stare at the wine glass as she filled a serving to the brim. "Yes," she responded after pouring the entire cup of red down her throat. The fire in her belly spread to her limbs and the heat escaped from her mouth. "You barely say anything to me at dinner on our anniversary but when you do, she is what you bring up?"

"I thought that was water under the bridge," Ben responded.

"It is, but I don't want you to take your dick out and piss in the river."

Ben was perplexed by the metaphor and rolled his eyes. That happened four years ago. And, as he

always said in his defense, it was one time and never
happened before or since with anyone else, though there
were always prospects available. Another impressively
full glass of wine was poured and consumed by
Bernadette; Ben knew the night could only get worse so
he poured himself an uncustomary third glass. "It's our
anniversary," was his reply when questioned whether he
thought getting drunk was a good idea.

"Just remember, you have to drive home. And
it's raining."

It's a shame there aren't any cliffs in downtown
DC, Ben thought while again nodding. The Potomac
wasn't too far, he continued to ponder while looking
southward in the direction of the water.

Silence prevailed inside the car once Bernadette
passed out mid-sentence. Rain pounded on the car's roof
and windshield. Quiet befitted Ben and the contents of
his head followed suit. The drive home was quick and
pleasant and when crossing the bridge into Virginia, the
thought of careening off the side and into the drink
never even crossed Ben's mind.

Restlessness was made volatile and exasperating by more drinking. Wine was replaced with whiskey at home. Several glasses ahead, Bernadette continued to drink the most. Passive insults started early; they began when pouring their first drinks. Ben's inability to "keep up" and also his stumbling after only a few small glasses of scotch were particularly noted. Through it all were constant jabs at Lizzie. The intensity of her tirade grew and where her words began as a defense of her behavior, they became more offensive with each mouthful of whiskey.

Nothing new for Ben. This was not their first battle and it certainly would not be the end of it. For the umpteenth time she wanted to air out laundry long since cleaned, folded and placed nicely in the closet. Better was expected from Bernadette on their thirtieth anniversary. Ben wanted a simpler evening that started with a pleasant dinner at a new restaurant, ending with a nice time in bed and if he was real lucky, a few chapters more from a book he hated to have to close. Instead, he was drunk and again catering to

Bernadette's alcohol induced insecurities about a subject already discussed to death and dissected.

The waitress *did* look like Lizzie, Ben was right. Even the way her bangs playfully fell over and partially covered her left eye reminded him of Lizzie.

"She really did look like her," Bernadette said, as if reading Ben's mind.

"Yeah. She really did."

"Are you thinking about her now?"

"I was, yes. Now I'm talking to you."

"Who would you rather be thinking about?"

"You, of course. It's our thirtieth anniversary." Ben moved with open arms towards where Bernadette stood but she maneuvered away with the excuse of needing another drink.

"But now you're thinking about her?" she said, her back turned and her tumbler filling quick.

"No. Now I'm talking to you."

135

Bernadette gulped the amber alcohol down, turned around and threw the glass against the wall furthest from where they stood. She spoke before Ben could register the action and protest. "For thirty fucking years I've had to listen to you and that zen bullshit. Where is your emotion? You never show any excitement, anywhere: not your face, not your words, not your actions...everything is always so passive with you."

To prove her right would upset Bernadette to furious heights so Ben stayed silent and exaggerated the usual reaction to his wife's verbal abuse. And to pour extra salt in the open wound, Ben turned his thoughts to Lizzie. Extra distance was added to the view of his inward gaze.

"Did you show any emotion when you fucked Lizzie? Could *she* make you do more than just lay there like you do the four times a year we have sex?"

Ben walked to the serving table where the half empty bottle of whiskey sat and picked it up, resisting the urge to break it against the wall. To both his and Bernadette's surprise, he put the bottle to his lips and tilted it upside down to take a hearty swig. Not a drop

spilled from the action. Before Bernadette started back

up, Ben held up a hand and repeated his previous

intimacy with the bottle, this time until it was empty. His

head started to ache and spin. "Now I'm ready."

"Then answer...whenever you're ready."

"That is an unfair question but I know you won't

give up until I do tell you so no. I don't think I did. Not

anymore than with you, I feel."

"Poor bitch. And poor choice of words. You *feel*?

That would be a first." Before she continued, Bernadette

found an unopened bottle of whiskey and claimed it as

her own. With a few mighty swigs she emptied a third of

the bottle. "I'm sure you didn't feel anything when we got

married, or had our children, or watched one of them

graduate from college and get married...you certainly

didn't act like it. Don't you think that's unusual?"

"No. I felt wonderful emotions during those

times, many other times as well. I'm just not as

expressive as someone like you-"

"Or at all!" Bernadette interrupted. "And what does that mean, *someone like me?*"

"Outwardly emotional."

Bernadette threw the bottle widely at Ben, missing on purpose. "Is that outwardly emotional enough for you?" she laughed.

Ben's response was to set the empty bottle he was still holding gently on the glass serving table behind him.

"Any other questions for me before I go to bed? My head is spinning and I want to lay down."

"Yes. One. I've asked before but maybe now that you're really drunk you'll give me a real answer."

"Well...?"

"Well...why? Why did you fuck Lizzie?"

"Honestly, it was the offer to try something different."

Tears spilled down Bernadette's cheeks; sadness was nowhere, only rage. "That's it?" She spoke through clenched teeth. Tension seized the entirety of her body.

"Plain and simple." Ben nodded off, comfortable in spite of his wife's mounting hostility.

"Do you know how many offers I've had to 'try something different?'"

"Many, I'm sure. You've always been beautiful." A quick nod asleep was retracted by an even faster upward jerking of his head.

"Yes! And I turned them all down! Maybe I should've fucked at least a couple of them just to see how that would make you *feel!*"

With all the force she could effectively collect, she launched her body at Ben. What seemed like the longest single blink of an eye in her life blocked out a moment of her trajectory. A fury of fists announced the real missile of her body. An actual tackle took Ben to the ground with his wife landing like a mess on top of him. The empty bottle fell and the ice bucket from the wobbling table followed and landed on Ben's head. Once Bernadette opened her eyes and saw it, she had an idea. She took the bottle by the neck and held it shaking, high above her head. Drunken strength brought the bottle down to a crash on the floor beside her. The broken and jagged glass jutting from the hilt of the bottle neck glistened in the dim overhead light. Equal vigor directed the weapon into Ben's shoulder.

Wide eyes peered wildly at Bernadette. A scream or even a whimper never followed. Brushing his wife off and aside was effortless with his unencumbered arm. "What the fuck are you doing?" Ben screamed, demanding to know. Bernadette got to her feet and smiled. There was some feeling, finally, in her husband's voice. All she had to do was hurt him. Another launch towards him brought a second successful strike to the opposite shoulder. Despite the blood from the previous wound, Ben used that arm to snatch the weapon from his wife. It garnered a confused look once in his possession before he threw it into a distant corner of the large living room.

The smell of blood filled Bernadette's nose. She was happy with the reactions her violence produced. Never was Ben so potent or impassioned. Heat emanated from between her legs and warmed first her thighs then calves. Sex with a battle wounded Ben possessed her thoughts.

With fury fueled by scotch and unphased by his wife's attack, Ben covered the few feet between himself and Bernadette with purpose and incredible speed. One step away from seizing her and his foot clipped the corner of a drink table. Face first he fell and toppled Bernadette as part of the process. A stinging open hand across his face brought all attention promptly to the present predicament. Their reactions were unexpected by each other and themselves. Ben was first; a well-delivered slap across his wife's face was the point of no return. The blow was meant to inform Bernadette that he would return any physical attack thrown his way. Bernadette's reaction showed no signs of understanding his intention. It was easy to push him off by catching him off guard with a follow up response of two hard palm strikes to the chest. What surprised them both was not her hitting him, it was the might and speed that threw Ben off and against a wall.

Slouched on his back and stunned, Ben's head throbbed in pain. A recollection of what brought him to the floor, flat on his back and bloody was impossible. The abruptness of Bernadette upon him meant that the time to figure anything out would have to come later. It was hard to see; Bernadette's head and hair eclipsed the already muted overhead light as her face hovered mere inches above his own. "Kiss me like you kissed Lizzie!"

The command needed no confirmation from Ben. Bernadette's lips forcefully pressed against his, nibbling and chewing and terrible. Her excitement was evident and slightly contagious. In Ben it manifested as a competition since only success truly aroused him. His teeth and mouth gnashed back at his wife's painted lips until the pigment was smeared and shared. Light traces of blood transferred to the shoulders of Bernadette's dress as she sank fully on top of her husband.

Ben's stimulation was stiff and eager. Excessive dampness from between his wife's legs soaked the crotch of his pants when she straddled him to sit upright. The smell of urine was strong until Bernadette stood up, removed her panties and threw them somewhere. Quickly, she fell back into a straddle on top of Ben. A dexterous hand freed his erection from the prison of natural fabrics and put it deep inside a warmer grip.

His head still pounded from the pain of contact and the flood of alcohol coursing through his veins. Still, a clarity was his alone and apparent from the glassy glaze that blinded his wife. Reality began to present itself in spite of the faint overhead light. First and foremost was a noticeable and red hand print on Bernadette's left shoulder. The shape and size matched his own perfectly. A wave of relief washed over him when he remembered then realized he hadn't slapped his wife's face at all during his retaliation. Black out drunk, Ben guessed and nearly laughed. Two superficial crimson marks were visible on his own shoulders when he saw the two reflecting stains on his wife. There was little pain to inform the severity of the wound and what little blood remained had dried. *Ice tongs!* Ben remembered snatching them from his wife after her second stab and staring at them, confused. "God only knows what she thought she was holding," Ben wondered.

"I bet Lizzie didn't fuck this good, did she?" Bernadette slurred.

Ben's answer was an orgasm. A quick succession of moans announced her own climax. When her breathing steadied Bernadette could effectively speak.

"How was that?"

"Perfect," Ben half lied.

Slowly adjusting to the state of the room, Bernadette's eyes narrowed for better assessment of the room's condition. An overturned table and empty, intact bottles were on the floor. Consciousness began to manifest in flashes, backwards from her orgasm to when she perceived was the moment of her own blackout. Embarrassment warmed her chest and arms as she sat next to her husband.

"Sorry about your dress."

"Don't apologize, please. I'm sorry about...everything."

"I'm sorry about Lizzie."

"You've already apologized for that. A lot. I'm sorry I'm still so angry about it."

Whether a blatant omission of the true trigger pulled or a genuine lapse in memory, Ben accepted the admission for all it was worth.

"We should shower and go to bed. We can clean up in the morning."

"My sentiments exactly," Ben agreed. He leaned over and gently kissed his wife. "I love you, Bernadette. Happy Anniversary."

"Happy Anniversary, Ben. I love you, too. So much."

She paused as she felt her cheeks become flushed and the wave of shame washed red all down her body. "Can you forgive me for all of this?"

"Just please don't do any of it again...except the last part, THAT we can do again!"

Bernadette smiled, ultimately. If it weren't for the carnage and soiling of the room and their bodies, her victory would lack the bitterness biting the sweet. Satisfaction came from knowing that he wanted to do it again and since this was a sentiment reserved only for her, she was the winner and Lizzie could finally be resigned as the loser.

Things That Keep Me Awake At Night

Dedicated to George Mitchell and Louis Broussard

and the thirty other casualties of the Upstairs Lounge Fire

in New Orleans, Louisiana, on June 24, 1973.

I am seeing a lot of purple. Clothes, neon lights, plastic drink containers, beads in a raucous array of pigmentation but purple seems to push its way through. Colorblind to a fault, I'm impressed I make it out so easily at night. Especially with the garish street lights making everything constantly shift hues. Time is shuffling its feet like the rest of the tourists in this city. No doubt they're affected and slowed by the heavy-handed heat plus whatever else mixes with it to keep the French Quarter languid and stuck in time.

This is the first time my feet are carrying me through the small, dirty streets of the Vieux Carré and everything is making my head spin: the smells of spices and coffee from kitchens, the bustle of people, the syncopation of jazz. These streets also hum from the currents of dead traffic; I know that even when I am walking by myself there are at least a couple spirits zig zagging through the crowds beside me. Even the halls and rooms of our hotel are choked with the souls of the slaves sold under a magnificent rotunda.

My boyfriend's family is an old one from the area with connections deeper and more tangled than the roots of the trees in the parks that break up the sidewalks and streets. He is the perfect guide and he is all mine. For the past couple of months our relationship has been tense. A lot of things we never took the time to talk about suddenly needed addressing. Through it all our future was never in jeopardy but our limits were certainly strained. New Orleans is our little vacation this year and a well-timed retreat from our troubles. Andy even took the liberty of not telling any of his family that he is in town. I'm grateful; more time for him and me.

It's been a couple of weeks since we had sex. Demands and stress kill my desire and I've never been the person to fuck away frustrations and worries. Much to Andy's dismay, I know that for sure. A necklace bought at a voodoo shop, an ornate key suspended between rows of white, pink, gold and blue beads, is said to be an offering in honor of Erzulie Freda, the lwa of beauty and love. Male homosexuals fall under her protection, so her graces are especially requested. The offering seems to be working; the entire time we've been here I've barely noticed many other guys but him, even after he points them out. I'm lucky to have him and he is the most beautiful man to me.

Wearing the lingering heat of the day well into the evening makes my skin fiery and tinged with red. The metal key on the necklace rhythmically taps my chest with its warming inspiration and assurance that supernatural forces are with us all the way. I am falling in love all over again while looking him up and down, remembering events or actions involving every part of that body walking fast to keep up with my hurried and long-legged stride. Perspiration crowns his brow to grant a more angelic quality. His kind eyes stare at me longingly as mine stare at him. Erzulie Freda's magic is unquestionably working.

Mutual lust becomes clear the more we walk, and the more I march I realize that my sweating is coming from desire. Andy's glistening came from exertion of force; as soon as we get back to the hotel room, I also plan on dripping from an explosion of energy. A knowing spark keeps shooting between us whenever our eyes meet, even if only for a second. A mere two blocks from the hotel. At the pace we're going, I'll momentarily be naked and in my lover's arms and soul.

Reaching for his hand comes naturally. When walking around Washington, DC it isn't uncommon for us to hold hands. Whether for a second or several minutes, I love this connection with my man. Also, I secretly like showing the world that he is mine and if he feels even half of the joy this brings me then I'm the luckiest man alive. My step gets lighter from the electricity of his touch and a sly smile wrinkles one corner of my mouth more than the other. If I'm upset or in a bad mood, grabbing his hand calms me and reminds me to breathe. High spirits are lifted stratospherically when our fingers interlock and we pull each other close.

Why, then, did he pull his hand away from mine? With my mind clamoring for reasons or explanations, my demeanor and energy shifts to abruptly turn sour. How am I supposed to react? We are in a well-lit area. There are plenty of people around, most of them families with children of various ages. It's only a little past nine o'clock. We aren't close to the drunken idiots of Bourbon Street. What is his problem?

Slowing down to give an answer made me realize I asked Andy the question out loud and he had heard me. "I just don't feel comfortable doing that here." I'm not satisfied with that answer I tell him and the look I know is coming does. Exasperation battling concern is the best way to describe it. Whichever wins depends on how upset he thinks his response will make me. No matter how he replies, I'm not going to understand. The motive becomes less important the more pissed I get.

The remainder of the walk back to the hotel is in silence. I look at any and everything else so I won't have to look at Andy. People have smiles on their faces from any number of things. The beer I had at dinner lost all its intoxicating properties minutes ago when my emotions sobered me up. A few things are said in my direction but I couldn't say what they were. Nod politely is all I could do. I don't care if that isn't the right response. Diplomatically committing to a peace for the

153

night is now crucial. I want to sleep a full eight hours for a change and going to bed right after getting to the room is the only way to make that happen. The extra time will be needed; I'm sure I'll still be a little too upset to fall right asleep.

****

My dream was very vivid. The sky was dark but not completely black. The sun had yet to entirely disappear but it offered no light, just a desperate red to mix with the deep blue of dusk. Jazz filled the air; clarinets harmonized with trumpets with guitars on one block and their rapture bled right into a different song from a similar combo the next block up the street. I was sure the axe man still happily walked the streets, finally and forever unable to ever strike again.

The French Quarter was different somehow. Buildings looked the same, but a couple of signs seemed unusual. I had no memory to go off of and in spite of the awareness of dreaming, it felt real and current. The smells were the same: coffee, spices, fish, urine. I stopped to take in all my eyes could see then closed them to clear my head from the overwhelming actuality of all the contradictory sensations. Opening my eyes after what felt like hours, I first noticed the style of dress was vastly different. Next, I could see outdated hairstyles worn beautifully by a variety of men and women. Confirmation number three came from the few vintage-looking but brand-new cars that toured the narrow lanes.

Street names and major landmarks were the same. The Hotel Monteleone was ever splendid and the guests still elegant. Ghosts also came walking through glass doors that weren't opened, wearing even older dress flourishing from exceptionally antiquated gestures. Nothing in particular was determining my direction so I went where the spirit moved me. Turning left on Iberville Street toward Chartres Street, I faintly heard a solo piano pounding out showtunes. Music to my gay ears. I followed until I was across the street from a corner building with a sign claiming an Upstairs Lounge. A faint buzzing noise could be heard from the bottom of the building near an

155

entrance. Would somebody answer the door? Everybody

in the vicinity meandered at a slower than usual tempo; it

must be Sunday evening. The seediness of the street

didn't quicken anyone's pace. This made it easy for me to

make out a man running from the direction of the bar.

Strange, I thought, since nobody else was in a hurry.

Screams shattered the peace and the calm

wouldn't return for several days. Chaos and panic

demanded the neighborhood's attention for just under

twenty minutes until the firefighters arrived and subdued

the flames. When the sky was clear of smoke it was

finally dark, that fire's light also extinguished. I woke up

after midnight with a smoldering sensation in the back of

my throat. Going back to sleep was hopeless. Any time I

would swallow water to wash more of the taste from my

mouth an apparition of two men in flames, huddled in an

embrace while melting together, would burst in my head.

An image like that is too jarring to forget and it would

haunt me for the rest of the weekend.

Weekend? Who am I kidding? It'll never really go

away.

****

Andy and I truly love each other. He's the first person I want to see when I wake up and the last face I want to think about as I drift off to sleep. This love for him is what's been keeping me going every day but it is also making me crazy. Approaching middle age has made me less keen on the idea of being alone but what if I can't afford the cost of constant companionship? Camaraderie is fine but I really need to better balance the time spent with him and time spent alone. What if I don't like the idea of looming expectation that he and I always arrive and leave together, to always BE together, physically? Living together is fine. Sleeping together is even better. Growing old together is comforting. Equating together was proving difficult.

Frustration propels my walking. I was pleasant during breakfast but quiet, briefly mentioning a bad dream and not sleeping well. How I'm able to sustain a hurried pace when also exhausted has always been a miracle to me. A sense of purpose, I guess. But I'm not sure what it is now. Most of the sights I've already seen and one slobby daytime drunk is the same as the one before. Out-running these thoughts presently is impossible when their embodiment is guiding me through the streets. A few times I think about deliberately taking the lead but it's worse for me to feel like I'm dragging a weight behind me. With him in front of me he could at least be eye candy.

I look at him and I see my future. One of my fears is that it'll all pass as briskly as we walk. How we walk, our usual manner of dashing through city streets, is also indicative of how we've both been hurrying through life. His focus is always on me and his worrying stems from what or how I'm doing, usually to his own detriment. My preoccupation is scurrying to get somewhere to do something. The more I think about it, the more I begin to realize I may not have any idea what I need to do if or when I ever get there. I know why I do it. And Andy knows why he does it. It's the same reason. It's for me, and I fear to our own detriment.

He is wanting to talk; his hazel eyes hide nothing. We are taking the same route back to the hotel and again my hand impulsively wants to lurch out and grab his to pull him close but I now know better. The day before, I rubbed his neck and even then he flinched and pulled away. Now it makes sense. I thought it was from his sunburn. The reaction is unsettling and I don't like it at all. I want to hold my man in public, to declare and display my love for him on his father's home soil but I'd be rejected. This would ruin my day more than it already has.

Hotel rooms always seem cold to me, even when it's hot outside and I want to cool down. The heat outside I prefer. There's less of an edge to me when I'm warm and relaxed.

"Can we talk?" He comes at me not even sixty seconds into the room with our shoes barely off, bags of books and souvenirs not even emptied.

"Sure, Andy. What's up?" I figure I have said all I can so my question is legitimate. What is left to discuss?

"You still seem mad."

"I'm just still confused. I understand your reason but I don't understand your fear-"

"It's just that-" His cutting me off is a failure. I continue since I need to get this off my chest.

"You're allowed to feel however you want and I have to respect it, but I don't understand it."

"I can explain-"

"How else can you explain?" It is my turn to cut him off so I keep steam rolling and regurgitate everything I have already heard from him on the subject. While I recount, the disappointment swells. "I'm even more upset with myself because I can't comprehend your rationale. You're constantly up my ass; at home, while I'm at work, even now while we're on vacation...and the more I think about it the more confused I get which pisses me off even more. If you want to be together so bad, why not start by holding my hand?"

Calming down is impossible. The hotel room is too small and suffocating. All I want to do is go back outside and walk around alone. That'll clear my head.

160

How easy will it be to convince Andy to let me go outside without him? Never in the form of a question since then it sounds like I'm asking permission. Once my intentions are stated, calmly so as not to upset him anymore, I slide on my shoes and head to the elevators.

Right on St. Louis Street, due northwest to Royal Street. Narrow streets are a blessing for pedestrians and the bane of drivers. A left on Royal Street toward the familiar area around the Hotel Monteleone. People are everywhere; laughing, drinking, talking and several openly dare to be in love. Streams of excitement and a purple glow come calling from Bourbon Street to my right; I came out to clear my head but can't, so I'll saturate it until I can't think at all.

Darkness and light dance harmoniously on the street, sidewalks, buildings and faces. Projections of sinful promises color our blank and impressionable faces. The weaker of us heed their call and succumb to the free-flowing spirits until they become possessed. Not me. The sense of being wanted is what I'm looking for. Drunken desire is still desire. If my man wouldn't hold my hand, it is comforting to know I can walk into the bar

I am approaching with rainbow flags lining the outside

balcony and several of the men inside would willingly do

more with me in public than just hold my hand. As

much as I want to hold somebody openly, daringly now, I

resist. Shame, considering the two bartenders I see

staring at me before I turn to go back in the opposite

direction. I'll quickly be at the hotel, back to a worrying

Andy and back into a confusing headspace that no

amount of discussion will bring me any closer to

understanding.

Recognizing Iberville, I turn left to put the

commotion of Bourbon Street behind me. Since this is

where I entered the chaos, hoping my own upsetting

clamor would get lost and join the rest of the noise, I'm

not really surprised to find it waiting to pick up our

dialogue exactly where we left off. For once, I think

getting drunk is the only plausible solution. Three beers

and I'm blitzed but I'm a happy drunk and happiness is

what I also miss knowing. The Hotel Monteleone is

coming up but washing my tears away with beer in the

Carousel Bar is a little uncouth and out of my league. I'll

keep walking. Restaurants and bars line the right side of the street so I cross to that side.

A sports bar on the corner appears welcoming. The cost of food looks promisingly low which suggests decent beer prices. This is confirmed with domestic beer listed just over two bucks. A laugh comes lurching out from the door and stops me at the threshold. The longer it lasts, the more its intonation and intention becomes a frightful, portentous wailing. The effect is unsettling; I don't want to go inside or even get drunk anymore. Without knowing precisely why, my feet lead me away. I want the company of my man, in whatever fashion he's comfortable with.

Light glints off something metal taking up nearly half of the sidewalk. Funny that I didn't notice it before. A preoccupation with getting out of my head kept that part of my body either level or tilted upward. All I can see in the dark is a triangle and small writing. Despite the people still out walking, I take out my phone for more light and try to read some of the small print. "At this site on June 24, 1973 in the Upstairs Lounge, these

163

thirty-two people lost their lives in the worst fire in New Orleans..." That's all I needed to read. Tears fill my eyes and spill down my cheeks along my nose. The saturation of my mustache seeps onto my lips and I welcome their saltiness in my mouth. When I swallow, an acrid taste reminds me of waking up this morning.

All the way back to the hotel I can't help but wonder why I've never heard anything about the arson. The more I think about it, the angrier I get. My mom raised me to respect the fighting and sacrificing her generation had to endure so that my boyfriend and I wouldn't have to be afraid to walk down the street holding hands. Does she even know what happened here a couple of days after her birthday in 1973? I'll ask her when I call tomorrow for our weekly Sunday phone call. I'm angry I didn't know about this tragedy. I'm furious that their lives were cut short at the beginning of our open struggle and forty years later it all seems in vain because Andy won't hold my hand in these very streets. But I'm most upset with myself for the way I've been acting.

Restlessness kept me awake but I'm not tired. Intentional noise is made to wake up Andy before his alarm. The insincerity of my apology is obvious just like the sense of duty effectively fueling me before my first cup of coffee at breakfast. Andy recognizes my impatience and coupled with yesterday's events and exchange I'm sure he's willingly complying so I don't get more upset. All he knows is that there is something important I need him to see. He's visibly relieved to learn that he's not the cause of my anxiety.

I take the lead when we leave the hotel restaurant. It didn't take long to remember the way, about the length of time it took to walk back last night. People are wandering from their rooms too but not enough to be a nuisance. Navigating the narrow sidewalks with purpose makes the few early idlers abruptly move out of our way. Before Andy could launch into what he read from the morning news feed, I stop.

"We're here," I say, then instruct him to read the plaque. After a few seconds, Andy looks at the door, back at the monument, then finally up at the building.

"What exactly is this?" he questions.

My answer is swift and catches Andy off guard. I grab him, a near bear hug partially around his arms to subdue any resistance and kiss him full on the lips. Thankfully he doesn't pull away. Instead his tension slackens and together with mine it melts and blows away when our kiss breaks and we exhale. I've missed holding him. I've wished for a kiss since yesterday that would tell him I love him, I'm sorry and so much more all at once. Without concern or permission, I take another kiss and to my relief his intensity and motivation rival my own.

"See? Just a few stares. No different than at home."

We share a smile and I know the rest of the day will be spent ecstatically next to the man I love. There's no need to hold his hand, though I take it upon myself to comment when I see other same sex-couples doing it. Respect can be shown to attitudes I can't understand, especially for Andy. The Gods know he tolerates and manages my many moods so now I understand. I want to be next to him all day; I want to be together with him for the rest of my life. We are one, our beings unified well before we moved in together.

There will be work to do at home concerning more independence and personal space, but that can wait for when we get back on Monday. It's only Saturday and we have nothing to do in the two days remaining but walk around, eat and watch people enjoy themselves in whatever fascinating way they see fit. Historical immersion or alcoholic submersion, any diversion was available and simple to find. For me it's being here with the man I love, mindful of the moment in his gentle presence. He's mine and I don't need to pull him around to show it off. As long as he knows, I'm lucky. And I plan on letting him know privately tonight and tomorrow night after once in the morning. And one more time Monday before we leave this harmony and start the week off holding each other like two lovers who will die still together, still in love, our arms binding even our ether as one on the other side.

Three Times One Equals Three

Thick, long, curly hair was abundant and could overfill both hands, no matter how much she grabbed. A fuller, harder body between her legs was another appreciated change. This body's musculature instructed it well and pleased Alonya. Not better; differently. Bearded kisses covered her face and she loved how she could smell and taste herself in the coarse hair around his mouth and chin. The difference of an extra man is what she came to love and not necessarily the man himself.

Under the guise of regular gym trips, Alonya's trysts were on Saturdays at eight. Sharp. Any other time she mentioned going to the gym, that's indeed what she did. But on Saturdays, while her husband slept in, she was out the door and in her lover's arms promptly by eight. Nothing out of the ordinary registered to either of them. This arrangement suited both of them fine.

Normalcy grew from the frequency of their encounters. But they happened in a house that was different from her own, that smelled different from her own and with a man that felt, acted and fucked distinct from Diego. These added up to a solution she felt was justifiable and conducive to her needs. Growing up in Saint Petersburg she always had two boyfriends. If one was unavailable or not up to the task, she had another option. One she would love more than the other. In her present situation, Diego was her primary man, her husband, after all. The other wasn't exactly inferior even though loved less and differently. It was a role the other was forced to accept while being based around an opinion that Alyona's husband would never understand, forced or otherwise.

Richard would meet Alyona at the door, completely naked and ready. He understood the importance of time; the value of each second was recognized and treasured. The hour she was his made Richard feel connected to more than himself or his job. Or even his new car. The automobile did only as it was told and couldn't love in return. His accounting job paid the bills and even though it was how he and Alyona crossed paths, it was empty also. Work didn't return nearly as much affection as it was given. And no matter how much he loved himself and his success, Richard

171

couldn't do for Richard what Alyona did, physically or mentally.

Near the end of their allotted time, the passion of their intimacy became pressing and immediate. Individual reasons for meeting had to be expressed and justified. A knowledge of what was necessary for each other meant habitual accomplishment. In a guttural growl, Alyona's shouting in Russian indicated her approach to climax. Quick, consecutive rocking replaced the slow and steady rhythm until she yelled, loud, his name. "Diego!" The Latin name clashed with their combined and mingled white skin. This still confused Richard's sensibilities since his blue eyes and chestnut hair mirrored his lover's as perfectly as their skin tones matched. Another forced acceptance for him. It was also the most unfair. "I don't want to accidentally say your name when I'm fucking my husband," Alyona said the first time it happened. "Insurance," she always said last, attempting hypnotically to convince herself.

After their first sexual encounter, Richard had wanted to ask Alyona to stay. Or to even visit him twice a week. Seeing her at work was torturous. Everybody knew about their relationship in the office, but these same people saw the enormous chunk of polished carbon hindering the circulation to her heart line. Fear of rejection in the form of a three-syllable name crammed any question back down his throat. The obvious acknowledgement and apology was always a brief frown and a deep, passionate kiss. "I'll see you at work Monday," was how Alyona said goodbye. But thankfully, it wasn't "Diego!" The name of his rightful rival. "Diego!" The name she credited for Richard's devotion and effort. "Diego!"

"DIEGO!"

Only a few miles away, closer to his wife than he knew, Diego wakes up every Saturday towards the end of the eight o'clock hour. He is awakened when, while dreaming, his name escapes Alyona's mouth on a whisper. His beautiful wife isn't beside him but she is still as fresh in his mind as her scent around the room. A smile completely Alyona's fault comes with him while he exits his subconscious. Warmth still lingers on her side of the bed. If only he could fall asleep again and rejoin his beautiful dream wife; the two of them perfect there, in life and in love.

Dreams in his case are stand-ins for real time desires. Alyona is always dressed in Diego's ill-informed notion of what a Russian peasant dress should be, something white and flowy. There, in his gray brain folds, where this fantasy is stored, Alyona is devoted to and dependent solely on him. Any need could be met by an ample and providing family wealth. Peruvian jungles obscured their grand estate in a lush, moist fog that could prevent one from seeing more than a few feet in any direction. Side by side was how Diego and his wife stayed since predators were a real threat in this illusory world.

His name was never called in vain. It could manifest as anything in his dreams, as a source of comfort or even the sole answer to any question he could ask. It sounded the sweetest when his wife spoke it while smiling. These three soft falling syllables were comforting to Diego in their own right. Alyona's saying it meant he

174

also belonged to her. But nothing at all like a complete reciprocal possession by true equals. Flipsides to dreams are telling, and the most concealed. What would Alyona think of her added role as a Saturday morning alarm clock? "She must be thinking about me," Diego would believe, wondering what body part she was exercising while all this went on in his head.

Schoolgirl Nervous

Schoolgirl nervous is how we both ended up describing the way we were feeling yesterday, anytime either of us thought about seeing each other again today. "It's been seven months!" became a proper chant. The first of a few apprehensions were eased after our phone conversation yesterday. He can be hard to gauge over the phone; he speaks in a similarly affectionless tone as me most of the time. But soon enough he'll be here and I can see for myself what's written all over his beautiful face while we interact.

He's been on my mind a lot lately and not just because we've been planning to meet here in Savannah for over three months. A tattoo on my right wrist reminds me of him every day. "Write on," the tattoo says, instructing me of my daily duty to the word and also my connection to him. A planned souvenir from the last time I was lucky enough to see him and hold him. Butterflies are dropping dead in my stomach as I watch and track his progress on my iPhone. I actually tensed up and shook my arms at one point when I saw how close he was. Just like a goofy fucking schoolgirl.

There's so much I want to say and will say. There are also so many things I need to say but never will. Not this time, anyway. Probably not anytime, knowing me. I'm too closed off and I've already made an ass of myself in front of him before, me acting like a jealous and lovesick adolescent schoolgirl. Wanting something from somebody who won't or can't give it is a predicament I am often successful in avoiding.

"I'm parking," the text from him reads.

"I'm already outside," is my response.

From the corner I can see both entrances to the parking garage. Families and couples spill out of the hotel, anything beyond that about them doesn't register. My notoriously one-track mind focuses on whatever singular objective I choose and for the past few days he has been the focal point. Trained eyes scour back and forth but I'm distracted with any new person who enters my field of vision.

I hate that he sees me first. By the time I turn around he is already staring at me, smiling. He was warned about what happens next. The mad sprint across

179

the street surely startles the people nearby and the kiss we share really seems to bother the valet crew. Low, sideways glances greet us and confirm my suspicions when we walk past them to enter the hotel. Never has anybody been more grateful for automatic doors than these guys, I imagine, and laugh out loud in their faces.

What do I do first? Words want to erupt, they want to form carefully crafted and practiced sentences. This sentiment is best expressed with a kiss. His lips are soft. Our scented beards mingle and I'm instantly more excited. Before what's happening registers, I take off first his shirt then mine. The aroma of his furry chest and belly instructs my desire and weakens me, sending me down to my knees. Every breath excels our hunger and without thought, fluid in motion, we shed our clothes like our anxieties and take refuge in the folds of each other's arms and bodies.

Staying in the hotel room with him and keeping him all to myself crosses my mind during our shower. So does having sex with him again but I abstain. We're both hungry and have been travelling too long to sit still.

Savannah is calling us outside; each of us hearing something different from the voice whispering through the trees decorated in Spanish moss. The short walk from the hotel to the coffee shop reveals much of the natural beauty offered by this oldest part of the city. Spots of warm sun speckle the pavement with glittering points of gold that shift shapes as a wind brushes the canopy of overhead leaves. Coffee from an old Southern queen more bitter than his envy pushes us through the heat of shaded streets, into bookstores and down towards the river walk. For him, he's experiencing this city as an adult for the first time. Eyebrows raise over his sunglasses in awe of the unaffected beauty our retreat offers this weekend. Green is everywhere in nature, grateful for the clear blue skies overhead. People laugh and drink openly while walking alone or as part of historic tours. Possibly haunted Italianate houses mix with Regency style houses certain of their spectral residents among other grandeurs around the more fashionable squares and streets. All this and more under a relentless sun burning bronze into our skin. The excitement for me is that I get to share this experience with him. Smiles and kisses reassure me of his appreciation. Does this mean he really loves me or are these tokens just his Georgia manners on display?

He has never been entirely mine for a single day. He will never be entirely mine. I have my reasons for thinking so, the biggest being my loving and understanding boyfriend. Another would be his boyfriend. Regardless, he's mine for two days. Every couple minutes consternation bubbles to the surface, the most buoyant being the question of whether or not he is as excited to be with me as I am to be with him. Or, on a grander scale, does he love me as much as I love him? I have two days to figure this out. Devising a way to extract information unknowingly isn't my style, anyway. Questions are meant to be asked. When nerves interfere with my ability to ask, then I observe and I'm often accurate in picking up on body language. The only concern I have is that with him my emotions tend to get in the way of usual rational thinking and behavior. Here goes nothing.

He is refreshing. I miss his company, the joy of being in his presence. I feel like I am the only thing that matters to him but within minutes it's crushing when a stream of distracting texts insist that I'm not. An extension of his right hand is his phone. A barrage of messages reminds me that other people think they're important, also. His boyfriend is the only person allowed to interrupt, in my opinion. Startling green eyes mean to tell me he's sorry when I show dismay. To me, they're mirrors exposing my insidious jealousy of whoever is imposing on my time with him, mocking me.

Seconds blur into minutes that fuel the hours of our first day together. I notice it only because I want to be in the moment and fully aware of how significant this time is for me. I hate that I'm losing minutes until I have to say goodbye, unsure of how long I'll have to wait before I see him again. The time will come, I know. Meanwhile, I refuse to ruin the present perfection with an uncomfortable inquiry. I remain steadfast in my dedication to be mindful of every word we exchange, every aching glance we share and every sensation I feel when I so much as touch his shoulder, let alone hold his hand. Even a second round of sex is more extraordinary because now I know the secret of how to keep him with me until the day he dies.

Awareness brings my attention to more than just fodder for personal pleasure. It's too easy to lose focus of purpose when beautiful green eyes aren't revealing my envy but instead stare back in approval of being wrapped up, naked, in bed with me. So far, that's the only way I've expressed my love. I don't count coffee, lunch or cocktails as a demonstration of love. Money can't buy his love, anyway. Thankfully he's not that shallow. I even decide to wait until he says "I love you" before I do. I'm always the first to say it and the first to feel the anxiety of waiting to see if it's reciprocated. I'm almost positive he doesn't take my declarations for granted but the way he reacts, or doesn't react, makes me wonder. Another hope I have is that by holding back my emotions and keeping them in check I'll be better prepared to study him while my eyes are unclouded.

I am earnestly shocked when he says those three words before I do. It never even got to the point where I figured I'd have to say it first because distance and time apart clearly must've made him forget. And he says it after the second round of sex that day. Not during, when endorphins and testosterone scream false claims in honor of orgasms. I respond with a smile, then a kiss and finally, I vocalize the sentiment. I want to kiss him again, longer, but I'm afraid of what I'll say or what might happen afterwards. The bed is now more of a mess and it needs cleaned up more than we do.

Gods please don't let there now be some obvious spring in my step. Keep any outward expressions of schoolgirl glee in check. He already thinks I'm goofy enough. And for fuck's sake, please don't let him know exactly how sweet I am on his goofy ass. I'm having genuine difficulty deciding how much of this giddiness is my excitement to see him versus how much I love him. Knowing me as well as I think I do, I'll say the scales might end up being a perfect balance.

Dinner and a ghost tour to go. Drinks in one hand while our others are united to lead us down sultry tree lined streets as the sun sets red to the west.

Savannah has always been a personal city and I'm cautious about who gets to share it with me. The new memories I'm making will forever be gorgeously framed by oak trees grown gray with pervasive Spanish moss. The food is fuel for learning local history and ghost stories, ending in one particular house. I smell cigar smoke in a room where no one has smoked in over a half century, at least. He gets bowled over when he enters the quarters of a slave who either killed herself or was murdered. This seals it for me. He and I share so many commonalities and now we have supernatural approval. His saying *I love you* first now seems more invigorating and reliable. The added acceptance of strangers is the perfect wrap up of the evening out with him. One lady even helps give a definition to what he is to me. "Let him get to his person," she demands of some stragglers choking a staircase when I'm impatiently seen trying to pass. We never know what to call each other so each other's *person* is sufficient and oddly fitting.

In his arms and between his legs feels more intimate. Our bodies are again connected, hermetically sealed and physically fastened – as above, so below. It's how I want to fall asleep but I don't want to have the bed changed again. I'm sure most of the staff is already annoyed by the faggots in room one-thirteen. I do fall asleep in his arms and the last thing I remember is how badly I want to be holding him when I start dreaming.

"Do you remember what you were dreaming about last night?" he inquires after a round of kisses.

"No," is my honest answer, "why?"

"You were fussing, saying 'stop it! and let me go!'"

"Why didn't you wake me up and tell me to shut the hell up?" I say in a failed attempt to feel better about my night terrors. It has no effect on the concerned face recounting the events.

"I tried. I put my hand on your arm and said your name. That calmed you down. You even sighed, like you were relieved."

The only valid reaction is a kiss. My appreciation makes it appropriate.

Another day with him all to myself and all I want to do is stare at him and memorize everything about the way he looks, the way he walks, the way he stands still. Why do his eyes visibly light up any time he smiles? How is it I am aware of this light no matter how far or close I am from its source? Mysteries keep secrets on purpose and the deeper I dive for answers the murkier and more forbidding the search becomes. It's always easier to just give up, accept the spectacle at face value and enjoy whatever escape and comfort it provides. The magic show is only good if you can't see how the illusionist crafts his tricks.

There's a story here, I tell myself in Flannery O'Connor's house. The story is one I'm terrified to write but I know I have to put it on paper. If it's too personal for the public, at least getting it out will be cathartic. A story or some written report was always half-expected, honestly. It might be the only way I can connect these disjointed fragments like dots and attempt some semblance of a bigger picture, to write my way through so I can better understand how and why he affects me the way he does when I see it all written down in black and white. Whenever I'm in another writer's house, this time with another writer, my mind starts waxing literary. I already know the title of this retelling but now I need to find its order, its reason. There has to be a better pretext other than a lovesick lament about how I don't have what I want and even if I did I wouldn't want to share.

Our last full day in Savannah is half spent and already I feel like I'll never see him again. I know I will but this is how bad it is, this phenomenon of a person, like time, slipping away and giving in again to the strains of distance. We've already picked out several dream houses to buy as possible writing retreats once one of us pens a bestseller. One or both of us will. I have more faith in him, honestly. But with the sun saying it's stretched goodbye, I charge him with what we do for the rest of the afternoon until we go to the gay bar tonight. Giving up that responsibility means I'll have more available gray cells for considering these past couple of days.

So far, his actions and words match in authenticity and at last, I feel a genuine acceptance and admiration from this man who forever has had me tied up in knots. Slack in the rope is comfortable and the complex loops loosen. With my hands free I can take the rest of the rope off my legs and from around my body. Once it's completely off, the bind loses its ferocity and captive powers. It's only then that I recognize my hands are beginning to reshape and refashion the rope from my prison into a noose.

Alcohol equals honesty and his words slap me across the face when they're heard over the pulsing bass of the music.

"We'd make terrible boyfriends, don't you think?" he says through a visibly ill at ease smile. I guess he's afraid of what I'll say in return. Or maybe he's just drunk. I'm afraid of what he's going to say next so I stumble through an inebriated agreement. I know my face can't hide the hurt that's twisting my insides. The noose is comfortable around my neck but I'm still not ready to jump.

"You're probably right," I say to both our astonishment. I'm not surprised that I don't know what the hell I'm saying next: words are coming out, I'm sure they're coherent but I don't like what I'm having to say. I hear myself agree when he says we'd probably end up killing each other. My bad acting works, I think. Whatever else I say elicits a response from him, thankfully. The words I want to say are choked back down and prevented from flowing out. The noose is also a tourniquet to keep me from bleeding out too many emotions.

I don't know what I want here anymore or what to expect, and it's driving me crazy. Will his thoughts be masked again by a sphinxlike smile and hypnotic, green eyes now that I've been led to believe one thing through earlier words and deeds? It's safer to laugh it off, to pretend I agree and hope to have a great time with the minimal hours we have left together. Can I now? Another beer will make me too honest and I don't want to make him worry. Better that I bear the brunt of the suffering, the wannabe martyr of forlorn faggots.

The second act of the drag show is colorful with a more complex light show than the first. An array of shades flash across our faces and I'd rather watch his expressions illuminated than the beautiful queens busting their asses for dollars. Each hue enhances certain characteristics in my beer addled brain and colorblind eyes. Not surprising that blue is my favorite but when green tints his face and arms, I like to think it's an outward manifestation of his secret jealousy. A deep green is prevalent during one performance. My hand reaches out and grabs his and a solidarity is felt and expressed in the identical green envious skin on my own arms.

Walks past the hour of midnight in historic Savannah are enchanting. With someone you love, the magic is twofold and exceptional. Crickets chirp in reaction to the lingering heat and humidity stifling the air. Overhead leaves dance and throw muted shadows on dark streets and sidewalks. Even dashed hopes and a slightly sunken heart can't break the spell of branches and gray moss swaying in the gentle breeze of a Georgia summer. Electricity still pulses when we hold hands. I know he loves me. I hope he always will. I know I'll always love him in some way, shape or form. This makes me feel more positive that he genuinely feels the same way. Impressions flood into me like lightning from the shared voltage ebbing and flowing between the connection of our joined hands. Concerns, anxieties, aspirations, fantasies, affections and affectations; all these and more are mirrored and strengthened by the reassurance of sharing. We have more in common than either of us could spend an eternity trying to put down on paper.

Early hours are for sleeping and I'm up well past my bedtime. He has a long drive back to Atlanta later today. My boyfriend will be here from Washington, D.C. in a few hours. We need sleep. Overwhelming me is the feeling that I need him more than I need rest. Desperation makes me want to hold him more because I'm still not entirely sure when I'll get to see him again. I get anxious every time I think about the other men who get to see him more often than I do and have easier access to his attention. Always wanting what I can't have is an endless merry-go-round: the constant spinning makes me sick but I stay on the ride knowing how easy it is to just get off the damn thing. No matter how much we talk about not letting months get away from us and grow in number, life dictates otherwise. Always one for signs, I see that we're wearing the same brand, color and style of underwear when we start to undress for bed. Only the design is slightly different. But the same glaring green color screams back at me, even in the dim light of the hotel room. This reflective reminder of my persistent jealousy is a slap in the face and spurs me into action.

His mouth kindly accepts my kisses, the sense of duty is noted but this time not fully appreciated. I'm disappointed but not deterred. His dick responds better so I focus on it but after a short while even it's too tired to return my friendliness. The customary wish of good luck he offered at the beginning of my attempt is now laughable. Luck was never on my side with him to begin with, I just now realize. This is further and final proof. One last time spent in each other's caresses isn't in the cards. What if we never get to see each other again? What if there are no more opportunities to be physical with each other? How much of what I want is actually unimportant to him? Now tired, defeated and depressed, only more pot will make me sleep since drunken sex is no longer an option. This concluding rejection means I need to reevaluate everything, even what I was thinking or feeling a few hours ago. Realizing I haven't come close to any real acceptance, conclusion, decision, not even any closer to him, is depressing. Realizing I was never fully sure of what I expected to realize is telling. Sinister doubts about everything I've felt or thought I came to know uncomfortably cradle me to sleep.

No reports of trouble when he wakes me up after a scant few hours of shut eye. I want to say how surprised I am by this fact considering everything racing through my mind, but I don't. We need to go pick up my boyfriend, which means whatever I was hoping to accomplish has failed. The execution suffered from my not knowing exactly what I needed to do, or even why. I'm sure I'll learn something once I'm a few days and a couple geographical states removed from this weekend.

Even his small talk on the way to the train station seems different to me. I wonder what he's really thinking. It's easy to dismiss the easy conversation with excuses of being exhausted but I think there's something else. I'm probably still projecting. Both of our guards are down, their fortifications are weak without caffeine. I swear I can see the same fear of going too far in the quick glances he gives me when he's comfortable with the stretch of road he's driving. There's the same agonizing hesitation in revealing too much only to lose so much in each other. I don't think I'm projecting anymore. Is what I want or feel anything close to what he wants or feels? Belief that he loves me is unshaking, but how shook is he? The vacation is now over.

Time heals all wounds, but time also waits for no man. Instead, it makes us suffer by insisting we attend its passing and not complain about the ravaging effects. In the case of a broken and bleeding heart like mine, time makes the pain worse by demanding the space between my friend and I be measured in miles, not only in months. I've also heard that time will tell, but if neither my friend or I can tell each other how we feel or what we really mean to one another, then time will be a catalyst for more uncertainty and secrets. I feel assured now that after all the internalized turmoil of this weekend, I have become a bit more understanding of my opinions. Jealousy isn't a new experience for me but I hardly feel it when I know I have to share. I've also never had to share a person with anybody else nor have I ever been on loan until now. But I'm almost positive that I can at least now gladly tell him anything he ever wanted to know about me and what I'm thinking whenever the questions or thoughts arise, if only he would ever take the time to ask or listen.

Acknowledgements

Thank you very much to all the people who read, re-read, then read again the stories in this collection and offered their invaluable feedback:

Christian Barnett, Cory Firestine, Diana Campbell, Shawn Hammer, Eric David Roman, Kyle Johnson, Nikki Drag

Thank you to Eric Melton for the many years of friendship and the amazing cover art.

Made in the USA
Middletown, DE
18 July 2020